PRAISE FOR THE JOHN ROCKNE MYSTERY SERIES

"As gritty as the Detroit streets where it's set, DEAD WOOD grabs you early on and doesn't let go. As fine a a debut as you'll come across this year, maybe any year."
—*Tom Schreck*

"From its opening lines, Dan Ames and his private eye novel DEAD WOOD recall early James Ellroy: a fresh attitude and voice and the heady rush of boundless yearning and ambition. Ames delivers a vivid evocation of time and place in a way that few debut authors achieve, nailing the essence of his chosen corner of high-tone Michigan. This is the first new private eye novel in a long time that just swept me along for the ride. Ames is definitely one to watch."
—*Craig McDonald, Edgar-nominated author*

"Dead Wood is a fast-paced, unpredictable mystery with an engaging narrator and a rich cast of original supporting characters."
—*Thomas Perry, Edgar-winning author*

Dan Ames' writing reminds me of the great thriller writers -- lean, mean, no nonsense prose that gets straight to the point and keeps you turning those pages."
—*Robert Gregory Browne*

KILLER GROOVE

KILLER GROOVE
(A Cooper & Rockne Mystery)

by

Dan Ames

Copyright © 2017 by Dan Ames

"Music hath charms to soothe the savage beast."
-William Congreve

KILLER GROOVE

1.

She shook it like she stole it
And I smacked it like I sold it
            -Topaz (by Groovy Train)

What had started out being a possible Top Ten drug and booze binge had rapidly turned into a Top Three. It wasn't the addition of more nose candy and Jack Daniels, but a strikingly sexy Blasian girl, Black and Asian for the less hip. Zack Hatter was certainly not of the less hip variety. In fact, for a guy his age, he was probably one of the hippest cats around. No one knew his real age, and Zack wasn't telling. Most pegged him around late sixties, early seventies.

Still, a Top Ten binge for the legendary Zack Hatter was worth alerting the press. After all, who else had gotten stoned with the Stones, plastered with Van Morrison and coked out of his mind with the Ramones? Zack Hatter. The Mad Hatter as they called him.

He was a legend, and not just in his own mind, although that was true, too. The Mad Hatter had always sported an ego the size of Montana, but his talent had backed it up. Until the drugs and booze and women had slowly siphoned off the magic that flew from his fingertips night after night, song after song. Oh, it still showed up occasionally, like a dim light bulb that occasionally glowed during a storm or a freak power surge. No one knew why, exactly, but the evidence was plain.

Now, his bleary blue eyes took in the sight of the crooked walls, gaps in the wood floor, and a ceiling with exposed wiring. He closed his eyes, the very ones that used to burn from the stage and turn young women's hearts to the mushy consistency of oatmeal.

"You're alive," the woman said. Her voice had a heavy accent and for a while, Zack couldn't place it.

Then he remembered.

He was in Mexico.

It used to be that when he had mornings like this, waking up with no idea of who he was or where he had washed up, he would be filled with a soul-killing sadness. A dread that he'd done it again. But the years had cured him of that feeling. It was a waste of time because deep down, he knew there would be more. So why trouble his soul with anguish? He had quit quitting a long time ago.

He was sure it was Mexico.

What was the name of the little town?

Bucerias, Mexico. A little fishing village devoid of all tourists but home to plenty of local drug dealers.

And it was cheap.

So was the girl.

He hoped. He couldn't remember what he'd paid for her.

Probably not much. Even blasted out of his skull, he never believed in overpaying for pussy.

Zack's brain and body screamed at him in agony. The hangover was like a freight train and his head was on rails, getting pummeled with each breath. His stomach roiled with acid and he would bet that before long he'd be emptying it orally.

His hands traveled down to his pockets looking for his cell phone and any cash. They were empty.

The only way to make a hangover even worse? Realize you lost all of your shit.

He looked over at a rickety table next to the bed. Nothing there but an empty bottle of tequila and a half-eaten, soggy shrimp. It was a sodden mass, hunkered down in a little pool of fluid.

Zack's belly groaned at the sight.

It reminded him of himself at the moment.

"What are you looking for, honey?" the woman asked.

He turned and saw her fully for the first time. She was old. Way too old. Probably as old as Zack himself, which he realized sounded awful, but he hadn't slept with a woman his own age in decades. Wait a minute he'd *never* slept with a woman his own age. That would be disgusting.

Zack could barely manage to look at her. Her skin was terrible and her teeth were even worse. Her face looked like it belonged to one of those poorly decorated skulls he'd seen at the tourist market.

"Mi dinero," he said. His words were barely audible even to himself. His tongue was swollen to twice its size and his mouth was dry and gritty. Like he'd swallowed a few buckets of beach sand.

The woman laughed.

Zack wasn't sure if she found his struggle to speak humorous, or worse, the idea that she had his money. He swung his feet from the bed and tried to sit up. The ground beneath him cantilevered and he nearly toppled over.

"Whoa," he said. This was definitely a top three.

Behind him, he heard the woman rattle some pills in a bottle, saw her take a couple of them.

"Por mi cabeza," she said, pointing to her head and wincing.

He doubted his ability to keep them down but he had to try. He spotted a half-empty beer bottle on the table by the door.

Zack stood, and lurched toward it, seeing through the window the Pacific Ocean, and the beach. Usually, an image triggered some vague memory of what he'd done the night before but this morning, nothing came. It was like he remembered who he was, and nothing more.

He made it to the table, grabbed the beer bottle then turned to the woman.

"What's your name?" he asked.

"Angela," she replied. "Your angel."

He tried to laugh but all that came out was a hoarse choking sound. "Angel?" he said. "Angel of death, more like it."

She walked toward him and shook some pills into her wrinkled hand. Angela held them out to him.

"What are these?" he asked, not really caring.

"Magic," she answered. The woman had to be messing with him. She probably made up her name and picked something she thought he would like. Who knew, maybe that was her tactic for getting him to go home with her.

"Si," she answered, even though he hadn't asked a question.

He popped the pills into his mouth and washed them down with the warm beer. He tasted cigarette ash and realized someone had put out their cigarette with the beer.

It didn't matter.

He swallowed the whole thing down, gagged a little, but clamped his mouth shut. Zack ground his jaws together, determined not to upchuck and he succeeded. Anything to take the pain and sickness away from him, however briefly it may turn out to be. It was a strategy he'd employed daily, even hourly, for a couple of decades.

He looked at the door.

"Buenos noches, senor," Angela said.

Good night? What the hell did that mean? It was goddamned morning.

He turned to ask her what she meant but the image of her was warped, like a fun house mirror.

Zack took a step toward the door but once again everything tilted at a crazy angle. And this time, it was joined by a creeping sensation of blackness at the edges of his vision.

Holy shit. He had to get the hell out of this place. Now.

He reached for the door and got ahold of the doorknob, but his fingers were unable to grasp it.

Zack stopped, felt a warmth emerge from his stomach where the pills from Angela had landed, and seep across his chest, up to his shoulders, down his arms and legs, and finally, to his head.

The door opened before him and he stepped through it, then realized he hadn't taken a step.

He had fallen.

The beach rushed up and smacked him in the face.

Gritty sand filled his mouth. His tongue kept rolling itself back up and trying to slide down his throat. Granules were in his nose and his eyes but he couldn't move anything.

All he could see was the morning sun rising and behind him, the girl talking to someone.

Maybe on a cell phone.

And then a black shadow crossed the bright sunlight and he wondered if it was some sort of magical eclipse.

As consciousness left him, he found one beaming ray of hope, the same final stray of positivity that had always found him in moments like this. The one thing that made mornings like this worthwhile in the end.

It was both a thought and a plan.

This was going to make a great song.

2.

I came from a town south of New Orleans
Music in the air and thievery in my genes.
                    -Frazzle (by Groovy Train)

"Well, I guess it's good that he's trying to do *something* constructive," Mary said. Her voice, usually full of sarcasm was instead this time replete with skepticism.

"Something constructive?" Mary's uncle, Kurt Cooper, looked at her, his face full of incredulity. "Are you freaking kidding me? My dude can wail!"

They were sitting at a table in the in the center of the banquet hall's main room, watching the stage where Jason Cooper, Mary's nephew, a pot-smoking young man with a seeming inability to find a steady job, was about to begin playing with his band.

They were called *Algae*.

The banquet hall was an old club near Hollywood that was now used mostly for old people playing Bingo, drug rehab meetings, and open mic nights where bands competed for a frozen turkey.

Mary sat at the plastic table with Uncle Kurt and her Aunt Alice. She was secretly wishing she had a Bingo card to pass the time.

"I for one am very excited to hear his music," Alice said. "I'm sure it's going to be a very entertaining show." And then she added, "One way or another."

Alice was a small, feisty woman whose husband had passed away years ago. She had the Cooper desire to take nothing seriously and matters of grave seriousness were met with inappropriate sarcasm. However, it seemed to Mary as if she was being sincere. Usually that type of behavior was frowned upon in the Cooper family.

"Very diplomatic," Mary said. "So unlike you."

"Does he write his own music?" Alice asked. Alice was a short woman, compact, who'd kept in good shape over the years.

Kurt shook his head. He didn't look so good for his years. Life hadn't been kind as his comedy career had never really gotten off the ground. He mostly worked retail jobs. Stocking shoes or stocking produce, he could hardly tell the difference anymore anyway.

"No, I asked him that," he responded. "He said he doesn't write his material. His material writes him."

Mary groaned out loud.

The band walked out onto the stage and Jason Cooper was the last to appear. Mary figured it was because he was trying to make a dramatic entrance or he had forgotten about the concert. Even money said it was the latter.

Jason had a guitar slung across his chest and his long brown hair hung over his face, half-covering his eyes. Mary knew he preferred that style to prevent it being obvious how high he always was. Of course, the smell of ganja came off him in waves so he wasn't fooling anyone, except for himself.

The drummer began to put down a beat. It was about as formulaic as you could get, Mary thought. She pictured it in a book for beginning rock drummers: Basic Rock Pattern #1.

The rest of the band members took their preordained spots with the bass player to the left side of the stage, the lead guitarist to the right, and Jason, the lead singer and rhythm guitarist, in the center.

He stepped up to the microphone.

"Here we go, baby," Kurt said. He clapped his hands together and leaned forward on the edge of his seat.

Jason opened his mouth and shouted, "I want to fuck you!"

Mary nearly spit out her beer and Kurt did a huge fist bump as the band launched into a wildly out of tune, out of rhythm song that sounded like something you hear when you drive by an auto salvage yard and the crusher is mashing a Ford Pinto.

As it turned out, those were the only intelligible lyrics Jason Cooper uttered. For the next ten minutes he and his band put on a musical display that made Mary want to wad up her cocktail napkin and jam the sodden paper into her ear canals.

"Are my ears bleeding?" Alice asked.

"Led Zeppelin can kiss my ass!" Kurt bellowed. He was bobbing his head, trying to match the discordant rhythm coming from the stage.

Mary got to her feet.

"Hey, where you going?" Kurt shouted at her. "They haven't taken their break yet."

Alice rolled her eyes. "The audience needs a break."

"I need to vomit," Mary answered.

She went to the back of the room where a portable bar had been set up. She asked for a Jack and Coke from the bartender, a guy who had to be ninety years old with his pants pulled up to his chest.

"Make it a double," she said. Mary pulled out her phone and saw that she had missed a call.

She stepped out of the concert hall into the lobby. The door shut behind her and she breathed a sigh of relief. Mary had never before appreciated the beauty of silence until she'd heard *Algae*.

The message in her voicemail was a prospective client – always a good thing, about a missing friend.

Missing persons cases weren't always her favorite, but provided the client's pockets were deep enough, could often times be very lucrative.

She called the number back.

Any excuse not to go back in and hear *Algae*.

Even the name. *Algae*. How had they decided on that?

She guessed Pond Scum had already been taken.

3.

There ain't no way to handle
There ain't no way to see
There ain't no way to brand it
When you scream out faithfully.
                    -Bareback blues (by Groovy Train)

"And now he's mocking me. That's the worst part."

I listened to my client and although I'd heard the same story many times before, I felt an especially strong sense of compassion for Judy Reynolds. She was a woman in her late forties with light brown hair and beautiful blue eyes. In fact, she was a beautiful woman, period. Slim, with an engaging face and a great smile. She worked full-time at the library, which made her even more attractive, in my opinion. Librarians were always a big turn-on for me. Not just because I loved books but because in high school, we'd had a total hottie as a librarian.

A blonde right out of college, as I recall.

And when I was in the library pretending to be studying, which I found myself doing a lot more once Miss Meyer started working there, I used to have some fairly elaborate fantasies about her teaching me the Dewey Decimal System, which seemed really dirty to me at the time.

"What exactly is he saying?" I asked Judy, forcing myself back to reality.

"That I'm a lifelong Grosse Pointer and now I'm living in the Cabbage Patch."

The Cabbage Patch was a section of Grosse Pointe closest to the Detroit border and home to mostly apartment buildings. If there was a section of the Pointes considered to be "poor," most would point to the Cabbage Patch. However, the area was really coming back, especially of late. New restaurants, a brewery, and an influx of medical students who went to Wayne State University, a short drive from GP.

"He's a shitbag," I said. Not maybe the most professional assessment, but honest at least. The fact was Judy's soon-to-be ex-husband was a real piece of work. "The work we did really nailed him and now you can focus on the future. Put him in the rearview mirror where he belongs."

Judy had hired me to find out if her husband was having an affair. It hadn't taken me long to discover that not only was he cheating, but he was doing it with multiple women and had been for years.

A sane person might ask how he was able to devote so much time to his infidelity.

That was easy.

Ol' Russ was unemployed. So when most people were at work, he was out chasing skirts as opposed to, you know, a job.

22

All of which put Judy in a tough spot in terms of getting spousal support. But the judge had taken the affairs into consideration and Judy had gotten most of the couple's savings that Russ hadn't been able to convert to cash.

"I want to thank you again for your help, John," she said. "I couldn't have gotten through this without you." She put her hand on mine and for a minute I was back in high school giddy over Miss Meyer. I think my breath even got a little shallow.

I cleared my throat. "I think you'll be fine now. Call me if you ever need anything."

Judy nodded, maybe blushed a little and used the awkward moment to cut me a check. As I was walking her to my door, it opened and a man appeared.

It was Clarence Barre, a former client of mine.

He stepped aside as Judy left.

"Hey, John," he said.

I shook his hand. "Clarence. Good to see you. Come in."

We sat on a couple of chairs in my waiting area.

"I can't believe how fast time has flown," I said. "How have you been?"

Clarence Barre was one of those guys – the kind they don't make any more. Big, ruggedly handsome, and with charisma to boot. He'd been a country music star for a few years back in the day, with a slew of hits. I had gotten to know him when he hired me to find out who murdered his daughter. I'd helped crack the case.

"I'm fine," he said, his voice deep and raw. He looked the same, a fine head of silver hair, jeans, a Western shirt with a black vest. Clarence had a presence. "Good days and bad days, I suppose," he continued. "As time passes, the good start to outnumber the bad."

He folded his hands across his chest.

"But I'm not here for me," he said. "It's about a friend of mine."

"Okay," I said. I grabbed a notepad and a pen from my desk. "Shoot."

"His name is Zack Hatter."

My eyebrows shot up. "Thee Zack Hatter? Of Groovy Train?"

Clarence smiled. "The one and only."

"Holy cow," I said. "Does he live here? In the area?"

"No, his home base is Los Angeles. Usually."

"What do you mean?"

"That's just it," Clarence said. "No one knows where the hell he is."

4.

You got to see it from a sunrise
You got to see he ain't no prize.
                    -Morning Vigil (by Groovy Train)

Ah, Bangkok.

His name was Rutger and he was an American, but he could have passed for virtually any nationality. He had the kind of look that wasn't a look. It was a style that lacked any substance, a blur in a crowd, a face instantly forgotten.

But one thing about him was obvious. He absolutely loved Bangkok.

He had a passion for its confusion. The chaos. The place where memories were instantly forgotten and no one told the truth. About themselves. About anything. Bangkok was a mystery wrapped in an enigma and then covered in a hot wet blanket applied by a nude teenager.

Rutger watched the band on stage in the little club, a group of five Asian guys who were playing Chuck Berry perfectly, note for note. The only thing they couldn't replicate was Chuck's voice, but even that was pretty damn good. They also couldn't imitate Chuck's signature moves like the duck walk and the splits. But then again, who could?

Rutger shook his glass – the last of a gin and tonic with some ice rattled around and shortly thereafter, a waitress appeared with a new glass. She put her hand on his shoulder and smiled at him. Not great teeth, but the classic slim body was ubiquitous and highly flexible. Rutger nodded back. He wasn't sure if the waitress was a man or a woman, but frankly, it didn't matter to him. His idea of fun wasn't dependent on what parts were available or not.

The band on stage took a break and Rutger looked around the room, his eyes never settling on any one face. The fat Canadian was still at his table, his red face sweating, another half-empty pitcher of beer in front of him. He'd been in the club for the better part of two hours and most of the barflies had made their best pitches to him but he hadn't made his buy.

Rutger knew what the Canadian was doing. The shopping aspect was the best part, looking at the products, rejecting most of them but keeping a few ranked in one's mind, always hoping a new, fresh face and hot body would show up and take the number one spot. It was all part of the process, one to be relished, not rushed. The anticipation was a big part of the game.

It was how things went in Bangkok.

Rutger saw the Canadian focus his attention on a woman wearing denim shorts with fishnet underneath. She had long black hair, a t-shirt with the bottom half cut away, and black boots.

Rutger immediately knew the Canadian had made his choice. It was written all over the man's face, and especially in his eyes. The pure, naked avarice was on full display.

Sure enough, the woman joined the man at his table and then the Canadian got to his feet, threw some money on the table and slipped his arm around the woman's tiny waist. They made their way to the door and when they'd left, Rutger stood, put his money on the table and followed.

On the street people jostled for position as the heat and humidity fell on Rutger like a wet blanket. He loved it, actually. He rarely sweat back home, even after one of his brutal workouts. But here in Bangkok, a long walk would leave him drenched. He could only imagine how the Canadian was faring, he could probably tail him just by following the sweat trail.

Like most sex tourists in Bangkok, the Canadian had chosen a hotel just a block from the go-go bars and clubs. Rutger saw him and his "date" disappear into the front of a mid-priced chain hotel.

Rutger waited a few minutes then went inside and found the hotel bar, making sure the Canadian hadn't stopped for a drink before going up to his room. Rutger ordered a light beer and left it untouched while he waited. He pictured the process up in the Canadian's room. The girl would probably want to get right down to business, but her customer would try to draw out the experience a bit to get his money's worth.

Several prostitutes approached Rutger but when he turned his cold eyes on them, they melted away. Rutger always suspected that the more primitive humans become in their quest for food and shelter, the more heightened their basic instincts become. Hookers, especially, seemed to sense that Rutger was a man to be left alone.

After about ten minutes, he paid for his still-full beer, took the elevator up to the 11th floor and walked to the door for Room 1159. A bribe of less than ten American dollars had bought him the information. The key had cost another fifty.

Rutger swiped the keycard, heard the door unlock, opened the door and stepped inside the Canadian's hotel room.

5.

It was a long walk to that hotel room on the edge
When the woman says a dark love is sacrilege.
                    -Tangerine Tango (by Groovy Train)

Mary checked the rearview mirror to see if her ears were bleeding. It would take days for her mind to recover from the noise of *Algae*. She knew right then and there she would never look at seaweed the same way.

The prospective client who had called her during the "performance," if you could call it that, was a woman named Connie Hapford. She had given Mary an address in Hollywood that turned out to be a neighborhood of mixed-use properties. There were apartment buildings thrown in with an odd array of shops and a few office buildings from the 1980s. The cornerstone of the area seemed to be a laundromat with a steady supply of foot traffic.

Mary parked on the street and rang the buzzer to Suite 2B, which on the office directory was listed as Groove Publishing.

The buzzer sounded and Mary stepped inside, climbed a flight of stairs, found 2B and opened the door. Inside, she saw a tiny waiting room with a table adorned with various music magazines. Rolling Stone. Guitar. Billboard. There was a worn love seat and a few framed gold records on the wall. She stepped closer to see the artist, but then a voice spoke to her.

"Miss Cooper?"

Mary turned and saw a woman clad in black leather from head to toe. She had a head of salt-and-pepper hair, cut short, and a knockout body. Her face was sharp around the edges and a few deep laugh lines could barely be seen. She was a beautiful woman who'd clearly lived plenty of life.

"Yes," Mary answered. "You can call me Mary."

"Hi, I'm Connie Hapford."

"Nice to meet you."

"Please, come back to my office."

Mary followed the woman to a single office at the end of the hallway with a large bank of windows looking out over Los Angeles. The floor was polished cement with a thick coat of polyurethane over it. The furniture was black leather and chrome. A few original pieces of artwork adorned the otherwise plain white walls. The air smelled faintly of perfume and coffee.

"Can I get you a coffee, water, anything?" Connie asked.

"No, thank you."

They both sat and Connie looked at Mary. A small smile appeared on her face.

"So you're a private investigator."

Mary smiled. "The best in Los Angeles, if I may say so myself. And what is it you do?"

"You must have some interesting stories," Connie said, ignoring Mary's question.

"I do, but right now I'm much more interested in your story," Mary said, neatly bouncing her prospective client's deflection back across the net.

"I'm in the music business. In several capacities," Connie said.

"Groove Publishing?" Mary asked. "That's your company?"

"Yes, that's my main endeavor. I own the rights to a lot of different kinds of music. I'm always on the lookout for new material, that's a big part of the job, too."

"Is it difficult to monitor your copyrighted material? Especially the digital stuff? I know people who rip off all kinds of stuff. Books, music, movies."

"It's a constant battle," Connie admitted. "But I have a firm who specializes in that kind of thing. They've got all kinds of alerts set up so that if one of my songs pops up somewhere, it should trigger some software. At least, that's the theory."

Mary knew that wasn't why she'd been called. It was something about a missing person. But she could already see how this was going to go. She was getting more and more involved in white collar crime and although she subcontracted a lot of that type of work, it paid well. Maybe it was more than one job.

"You've probably got a lot of stories to tell, too," Mary said, sensing that maybe Connie wasn't quite ready to get to the matter at hand.

"Oh, a few. But they're mostly old stories. My life these days is pretty boring in comparison."

Mary nodded and waited. Some clients liked to get right to the point. Others liked to beat around the bush for a while, but those were usually the highly personal cases. A cheating spouse and the cuckolded party couldn't bring themselves to broach the subject.

Mary had a pretty good idea that Connie was about to get to the point.

And she did.

"Have you heard of Zack Hatter?"

"Sure," Mary said. "He was the lead singer for Groovy Train."

Mary remembered the band. A somewhat legendary blues-rock group with quite a few big hits, a lot of albums, and fans from several generations. They were America's lesser-known version of the Rolling Stones. Most critics had dismissed them at the time, but over the years their reputation had actually improved.

"Yes. He was and still is, technically. Anyway, he's gone missing."

A smirk couldn't help but put itself on Mary's face. "From what I've heard," Mary said, "Mr. Hatter has a propensity for disappearing from time to time." She was referring to the many tabloid stories about Zack Hatter's love of booze, drugs and women. That passion was often coupled with an open disdain for authority.

The expression on Connie's face told Mary she was right. "Yes, that's true. He's battled every kind of substance abuse known to human beings, and that journey has caused him to take extended absences from the public eye."

Connie's shoulders had slumped and some of the life had gone from her face. Mary knew worry when she saw it. And this was personal.

"I take it this one isn't just a public disappearance, but a private one, too?" Mary guessed. "Hence the need to call a private investigator."

"I'm afraid you're right," Connie said.

"What's different about this one?" Mary said. She pulled a small notebook and pen from her purse.

Connie sighed and looked out the windows. A haze hung over the horizon and Mary saw the woman's reflection in the glass.

"This time, he didn't just disappear," she said. "He was kidnapped."

6.

Borrowed a Rolls from a guy down the street
Came with champagne and the sound of running feet.
         -No Bitch (by Groovy Train)

I parked the car in my driveway and was about
to open the door when my cell phone rang. I glanced
down and saw it was a call from Las Vegas. I don't
get many calls from Vegas. In fact, it might have been
the very first one I'd ever received in my life.

"Hello?" I answered.

"Is this John Rockne? The detective?" It was an
older man with a grizzled voice.

"This is John Rockne, the private investigator," I
answered. "Who is this?"

"This is Wayne DeGraw," the man said. "My
buddy, Clarence Barre said he was going to talk to
you about our missing friend."

After Clarence Barre had told me about Zack Hatter and how he'd gone missing, he'd told me that the actual guy who wanted to hire me would be calling. I'd been slightly disappointed in that I liked and respected Clarence Barre and had been hoping I would be working for him. But in my business, you can't always choose who's going to hire you.

"Yes, that's right, Mr. DeGraw," I said. "Clarence just filled me in on what few details he had."

"Hey, man, call me Wayne." He sounded like a refugee from the sixties, which might not have been a bad guess.

"Okay, Wayne," I said. "Yes, I talked to Clarence and he said you were going to give me a call. You're the one who discovered Zack Hatter was missing, right?"

I got out my notepad and pen. In the living room window, I saw one of my daughters peek out at me. I did a finger wave.

"I wouldn't put it that way," Wayne said. "I don't really know if he's missing or not. I'm sure Clarence told you all about Zack, right?"

"More or less. He's still living the lifestyle of a rock star, right?"

"Yeah, that crazy ass just never stopped. So there have been times when he's been hard to reach, man. Real hard. But usually you just go down to the local bars and ask where the loose women are and eventually you find him. But none of that has worked and it's been at least a month since anyone's seen him. That's a pretty long time, even for Zack."

I saw the back door of my house open and my wife leaned over the railing and looked at me. I pointed at the phone in my hand and she gave me the ok sign.

"Why don't you start from the beginning?" I asked. "How did you know Zack?"

"I was a roadie for Groovy Train for almost twenty years. I was the only one around who could keep up with him. In terms of booze and…the other stuff, you know what I mean, man?" I heard Wayne take a deep breath and then a slow exhale, and could picture him smoking a cigarette on the other end of the line.

"Got it."

"Anyway, we've kept in touch over the years and when his family can't find him, they usually hire me to go drag him out of who-knows-where and sometimes into rehab. That sort of used to be my job back in the day."

"I see."

"So this time I traced him to Mexico, but after that, nothing. And like I told the family, and Clarence, this time it really feels like something bad happened."

"You say, Zack's family. Who are you talking about?"

"His ex-wife and their two kids. A son and a daughter. They still live in LA."

Los Angeles. Mexico. This was really starting to feel like something outside of my capabilities. I had agreed to at least talk to Wayne as a favor for my old client Clarence. But now I felt the need to be blunt.

"Look, Mr. DeGraw."

"I told you to call me Wayne, man. I think you're lookin' for my old man when you say Mr. DeGraw. And good luck finding that crotchedy old bastard!"

What followed was a racking cough that sounded like a punctured antique accordion.

"Okay, Wayne. Look, if you or the family think there is foul play involved you really ought to call the police. And if they can't help you and you really feel the need to hire a private investigator, there are dozens of firms in Los Angeles, or Las Vegas, who can help you. I'm in Grosse Pointe, a suburb of Detroit. I'm not sure how I can help you."

"You come highly recommended by Clarence. You caught the guy who killed his daughter, right?"

"I think that's simplifying it a bit," I said. "But generally, yes, that's accurate."

"Look, we already talked to the fuzz in LA and they can't help us."

The fuzz?

"And since he disappeared in Mexico, no one else wants to help, either. Plus, Zack's reputation precedes itself, you know what I mean? An old rock star with a taste for booze, drugs and loose women, lost in Mexico? It ain't like Johnny Law is gonna put a team of detectives on it. In fact, *they* told the family to hire a private investigator. But they didn't know who to call so they asked me, and I remembered Clarence had said you came through in the clutch, man."

Now I felt like an ass.

"If nothing else, you have to consider the expenses," I said. "I would have to, at some point, probably fly to Los Angeles and then to Mexico. We're talking a hotel room, rental car, expense money if I have to grease the wheels with anyone. And that's all in addition to my day rate. That's a lot of money," I said. And then added, "Man."

I heard DeGraw snort on the other end of the line.

"Zack's ex is rolling in dough, buddy," he said. "A couple of years ago I think they let someone use one of their songs for like a few million bucks. Might have been for a feminine wash product or something. A douche. Can you believe that, man?"

"There's big money in vaginal cleaners," I said.

"Look, bro, tell me what you have in mind if you took the case," Wayne said. "And I'll call the family and then get back to you."

Just to be safe, I estimated on the high side what it would cost for me to get involved and DeGraw thanked me. He seemed unfazed by my number. Maybe he was used to rock 'n roll sized budgets. We disconnected and I got out of the car and went inside my house.

My wife looked at me.

"Feel like going to Mexico?" I asked.

7.

The promise fell on my shoulders
The truth landed over the trees
From a voice of wayward angels
On their way to my gentle reprise.
              -Midnight Truth (by Groovy Train)

"What...?" the Canadian managed to stutter before Rutger shot him. The bullets, two of them, hit the surprised man in the center of the forehead with just a sliver of a gap between the two entry wounds.

Rutger was also surprised, albeit a bit more pleasantly than his victim.

The gun in his hand with a curlicue of smoke rising from the muzzle was a knock off. A semi-automatic made by the legendary illegal gunsmiths of Cambodia. They lived in the mountains and did the entire fabrication in little villages almost solely dependent on the illegal gun trade. They used crude templates and primitive techniques, but the guns worked well.

The silencer also worked well, the sound had been no more than a polite cough. That had been easier to purchase, a quick twenty bucks on the street, about a dozen blocks from the hotel.

The Canadian, whose real name was Thomas Strang, fell backward onto the hotel floor, half of his head missing. Mr. Strang had chosen to embezzle from the wrong people and now Rutger had taken him to task, once and for all.

The hooker, Rutger decided, had been a fairly good choice. She was quite striking, with great skin, long legs and fairly large breasts that looked natural.

She also had a strong survival instinct, which prevented her from screaming. She was still on her knees at the foot of the bed. She didn't look scared, just wary.

If she had chosen to break into hysterics, Rutger would have shot her. Instead, he lowered the gun and stepped toward the bed. Mr. Strang had apparently been into at least a little bit of S&M because there was a set of leather handcuffs and a ball gag on the bed.

Rutger lifted the ball gag harness with the muzzle of his gun and flipped it toward the hooker.

"Put this on," he said.

For the next two hours he did to the hooker what the Canadian had most likely been fantasizing about for most of his life.

In the end, Rutger killed her anyway. She had seen him. Seen him kill Thomas Strang and couldn't be trusted to keep her mouth shut.

Rutger wiped the gun clean and put it in Strang's hand and carefully pressed the dead man's fingers onto the metal, making sure some very clear prints would be left for the authorities in Bangkok. Not that the authorities were really anything to worry about. They were slow, ineffective, and legendary for accepting bribes.

So he wasn't worried in the least, but he was hungry. It never ceased to amaze him what killing and screwing did for the appetite.

Rutger thought about it, but room service wasn't an option. Oh well, he thought. He would have to get something on the way to the airport.

He double-checked the message on his phone.

Hurry home, it said. Important job. Double scale.

Other than a Thai whore strapped to a bed, nothing excited Rutger more than a job that paid twice his normal fee.

Sure, it would be a lot more dangerous, but he liked it that way.

No guts, no glory.

8.

Pass me that bottle
Roll me that joint
Say what you want
Remind me of your point.
                -Short Boys (by Groovy Train)

"What do you mean kidnapped?" Mary asked.

Outside, Mary saw an airplane take a wide path over the Pacific before banking south toward LAX.

"I don't know for sure," Connie Hapford said. "But he's never disappeared quite like this. He's gone missing for long weekends or even sometimes for multiple weeks. But even then, there were always sightings, especially on social media. People love to get their picture taken with Zack and then post it on Facebook. Half the time we could follow Zack's drunken journeys on Facebook and Twitter."

Connie sighed and Mary thought she heard the woman's leather outfit sigh, too.

"But to literally fall off the face of the earth and for no one to know where he is or to have seen him for this long leads me to believe somebody grabbed him," Connie continued. "And, frankly, no one has ever accused me of being creative so I don't think I'm acting like a conspiracy theorist."

Mary considered that. And then she asked, "Why would anybody want to kidnap Zack? For you to go right to the kidnapping theory means there's a chance you know someone who might want to grab him."

Connie stood and her leather pants made a creaking sound. It made Mary think of an old Western where the rider adjusted himself in the saddle.

"No, I don't," Connie said. "I can't really think of anyone who would want to abduct him. For Christ's sake the man is a handful. Like, if you were going to choose one grown man to babysit, it would not be Zack Hatter. He's a train wreck never more than one step from going off the rails."

Mary could tell there was a fair amount of personal history there.

"How wealthy is he?" Mary asked. "Is he one of those mega wealthy rock stars like Mick Jagger? Or did he piss away everything he owned?"

Connie shrugged.

Mary continued. "What I mean is, does someone think there's a huge ransom at stake? That they've hit the jackpot? Or should I say Zackpot?"

Not even a smile from her client. "Zack had a saying," Connie replied, "that he spent his money on booze, drugs and women. The rest of it he wasted."

That sounded about right to Mary, in terms of all the stories she'd heard about Groovy Train. When they were on tour, the concerts only served to break up the partying.

43

"So what does he do now?" Mary asked. "I know Groovy Train isn't touring any more. Is Zack? Does he do any recording? Or is he riding on his royalties, kicked back on a beach, sucking down booze and getting skin cancer?"

"He still tours, albeit haphazardly," Connie said. "He still writes music but he hasn't had any of the kind of success that Groovy Train had. As far as how he spends his time, who knows? The man careens from one place to another, from one party to the next. Hell, even he doesn't know where he is half the time."

Mary figured it was time to 'manage client expectations' as a speaker at a private investigator seminar once said. In fact, if she recalled it was an entire section in his PowerPoint. Or maybe not, she had fallen asleep during his speech. One too many cocktails at the free lunch.

"I'm going to caution you against going straight to the kidnapping angle," she said to Connie. "In a case like this, with a subject like Zack Hatter, it could be that he fell off of a cliff or maybe he booked a flight to Australia and he's wandering around the Outback with a guide, hunting alligators and pretending to be Crocodile Dundee. Who knows?"

Connie tilted her head to one side as if she was struggling with the content of what Mary had just said. "Those are all possibilities, I have to admit," she said. "I just threw kidnapping out there as a possibility. It wasn't like I was suggesting that was the only option. With Zack, there are always multiple scenarios in play."

"Okay," Mary said, deciding to be blunt. "May I ask why are you so interested in Zack's disappearance and what exactly do you want me to do about it?"

Connie sat back down behind her desk. "Okay, here's the deal," she said. "I own the rights to some Groovy Train songs. It's a long story but Zack and I were an item back in the day and he needed some money pretty badly. Some people claim I took advantage of him but I saw it as an investment, pure and simple."

"And did the investment pay off well?"

"It did," Connie admitted. "Those rights are very lucrative, however, they are renewed every five years so I personally need Zach Hatter to be around for a while longer."

"And how far are we from the end of the current five-year period?" Mary asked.

"About two months."

"I see," Mary said. It was her favorite time period when landing a new client. The moment when everyone was at least starting to get down to brass tacks. When some of the bullshit came to a stop.

"So why don't you tell me your rates," Connie said. "And I'll give you all of his contact information as well as the names and phone numbers of people who maybe knew where he went."

Mary thought it was funny that Connie just assumed she would take the case. She thought about putting up the pretense of needing some time to think about it. But then she would be the one bullshitting. She wanted to take the case. Not only did it have a chance to be profitable, it could be interesting and maybe even a little bit of fun. So she went over her rates and then said to Connie, "And you think his last known whereabouts was somewhere in Mexico?"

"That's what I heard," Connie said with very little confidence. "By the way, you come highly recommended," she added. Connie mentioned the name of an entertainment lawyer who had used Mary many times and whom she'd never disappointed. "When can you get started?"

Mary thought about it and considered her somewhat light-in-the-loafers caseload and told Connie she could start immediately.

They shook hands and Mary detected a faint but unmistakable scent.

The leather outfit must have been purchased recently. It still had that new-car smell.

9.

She was a wild-eyed girl just north of seventeen
A smile like the wind and eyes ain't never been seen.
                    -Gone Girl Yesterday (by Groovy Train)

"Are you out of your mind?" my wife asked me. Anna Rockne had actually been born Anna Giordano and the fire in her dark eyes belied her Italian heritage's reputation for a temper that's quick on the draw.

"Quite the contrary," I said. "I've never felt more sane."

"You?" she said, eyes still flashing like twin muzzles on a double-barreled shotgun. "Chasing someone down in Mexico? Give me a break, John," she said. "I could see you landing in a Mexican prison within a day or two, and those guys would love to get their hands on some sweet Gringo ass like yours."

I shook my head. "First off, thank you for the compliment regarding my level of physical attraction. I've been doing a lot of squats lately at the gym just for that reason. But I must say I'm a bit disappointed in your lack of confidence."

"Seriously?" Anna asked. "Do you even speak any Spanish? Remember what happened when Butch Cassidy and the Sundance Kid went to Mexico?"

"Wasn't that Argentina?"

"Whatever."

"I've been brushing up on my Spanish lately," I said. "Cerveza. Tequila. Burrito. Señorita."

"How do you say Dead Gringo in Spanish?"

"I don't know. That wasn't in my textbook."

Anna and I had been married for over ten years and we had two daughters, Isabel and Nina. The girls were upstairs doing their homework, and I was trying to explain to my wife how the case of the missing Zack Hatter wouldn't be dangerous. Okay, more honestly, I was downplaying the inherent risks in pursuing anyone in Mexico. Or Los Angeles for that matter.

"First off, I won't be going right to Mexico," I said. "I'll start, as always, by working the phones and the Internet. And if I did have to travel, the first trip would be to Los Angeles, not Mexico. And they still speak English in Los Angeles, I'm pretty sure."

"All of your travel expenses would be paid for?"

"Yes, I included those in my estimate."

We were sitting in the living room, opposite one another. Anna was on the couch with a glass of red wine, I was in one of our chairs with a bottle of beer.

"Gosh, I wish I could come," she said, her tone softening and I felt like a Florida house still standing after the hurricane passed by. "But there's no way with the girls and school."

To be honest, it sounded like fun to make it a family trip, but I knew it wasn't practical.

"Maybe I'll have Zack write an autograph to you, once I find him," I said. I knew that Anna at some point had listened to and liked Groovy Train's music.

"You sound pretty confident," she said.

"I'm a professional," I said.

"A professional smart-ass," Anna observed.

There was a soft knock on the back door and then I heard someone come in, grab a bottle of beer from the fridge, pop the cap and come into the living room.

It was a cop.

And not just any cop.

But the Grosse Pointe Chief of Police.

"Look at you two, sitting around drinking once again," the cop said. Her name was Ellen Rockne. My big sister.

"John is going to try to find Zack Hatter, the lead singer of Groovy Train," Anna said. "Last seen somewhere in Mexico."

My sister looked at me, then back at Anna.

"John in a Mexican prison?" Ellen let out a low whistle. "That's gonna hurt. That's gonna hurt real bad."

10.

You always fade away into the background.
A thousand memories of you never around.
                    -Morning Lies (Groovy Train)

On the way back to her office after meeting with Connie, Mary dug through her iTunes library on her phone and found a Groovy Train album. She set it to play, using the Bluetooth to send it through the car's audio system.

As the blues-rock-funk beat filled her car, Mary found her foot tapping along to the music.

It was a song called Palm Girl Blues.

I met her on an island called the Cast Away
Hard shell soft skin smokin' and drinkin' all day
She said the island wasn't no place for a man like me
Then the words were in the wind and so were we

Mary wondered about the magic of songwriting. She'd heard once that Ronnie Van Zant, the lead singer and songwriter of Lynyrd Skynyrd never physically wrote down a single lyric his whole life. He carried the songs around in his head.

She thought about Zack Hatter and realized that if he did the same thing, he could potentially have a fair amount of money sloshing around in his whiskey-soaked brain.

Enough for someone to kidnap him?

Maybe.

More likely, though, if it was a kidnapping it was straight up about ransom. Having nothing to do with Hatter's musical ability and inclinations. Just a guess, but Mexican kidnappers were pretty straightforward people. We've got someone you care about. Send us money, or we put a bullet in their head and bury them in a shallow grave.

End of kidnapping scheme.

Still, Mary was having a hard time even getting to the idea of a kidnapping. The guy was a rock star well past his prime, legendary for alcohol and drug use. He'd even disappeared multiple times before.

A kidnapping seemed like someone's overactive imagination going into full overdrive.

The cynical part of her realized she could make a fair amount of money thanks to that turbocharged paranoia. The realist in her said the case would most likely be closed fairly quickly and painlessly.

She pulled into her parking space next to the building that housed her office. It was on Main Street in Venice, along a row of trendy shops and restaurants where it wasn't uncommon to see a celebrity slumming it to their latest yoga class. Now, it was fairly quiet with a few tourists doing some window shopping. The famous southern California sun was out and its warmth felt good on Mary's shoulders. She made a mental note to try to fit in a beach day one of these weekends, but the problem with owning your own business was that there was always work to be done.

Mary took the stairs to her office, unlocked the door and went inside. She set her phone on the desk next to her computer and roused it from its sleep, and then opened up a new folder called simply "Hatter."

She typed up a field report of sorts detailing her interview with Connie, and then she entered the information on Zack's acquaintances into both the document and her phone.

Who to call first?

That was easy.

You always have to start with the ex-wife.

Mary punched in the number, which was the first one listed on the information sheet given to her by her client.

While she waited, Mary found herself humming the melody of Palm Girl Blues.

Damn, she thought. *Zack Hatter knew how to put a song together.*

11.

Ain't no booze never been my friend
Ain't no lies I been too afraid to lend
Pass me the bottle, draw me a line
Whisper in my ear like you do every time.
                    -Lime and Coke (Groovy Train)

Alive.
The Hatter was alive.
He thought of the song from Pearl Jam.
And giggled.
And cackled.
And drooled.
The Mad Hatter was delirious, he half-realized. Or should he say, The Mad Hatter was Mad? As in looney tunes Mad?

His body craved a million different substances and in the dark, every shadow was a personification of Satan coming to flay him for all of his past evil deads. Deads? Deads! He meant deeds!

Shit!

A deep convulsion shook his body and his legs twitched. He couldn't breathe. When it finally passed, he gasped.

And then giggled.

What a great idea for a song.

Evil Deads!

Or, wait a minute, wouldn't Satan reward him for evil deeds?

The Mad Hatter cackled again.

He couldn't keep his fake gods straight.

There was a loud bang and the Hatter jumped. And twitched. His body was racked with the shakes.

Holy shit! Was that a gunshot?

Fuck, he wished he had a pen and paper. The lyrics to Evil Deads were coming to him wrapped in cravings for booze and pills.

He needed a double shot of tequila with a Valium and maybe a Percocet.

An explosion of light shattered his thoughts and blinded him.

The Hatter squeezed his eyes shut but a reverse negative image of a shadow standing in a doorway pressed itself into his shuddering mass of a brain. The image was of a person, he couldn't tell if it was male or female, with a bottle in one hand, and a goddamned machete in the other.

The Mad Hatter laughed, whimpered and started crying.

A goddamned machete! His brain hissed. What the fuck did they need a machete for? Chop off his head? Why? What did they need his head for? Did someone ask for some head and the original meaning was lost in the translation?

The Hatter giggled, shook and giggled again.

He heard footsteps right in front of him but he refused to open his eyes. It was better not to see!

And then his body tensed until he thought he would snap like a guitar string, when suddenly every muscle in his body relaxed, like air being let out of a balloon.

An awful odor assailed his nostrils and he realized he had shit himself.

Evil deads!

12.

That old man he's a helluva lost cause
Eyes that'll hate you never feel your claws.
*   -Shrug It Off (by Groovy Train)*

After a night of fitful sleep in which I was passed around a Mexican prison like a library book, I got up early, showered and went to my office. My prize of the day was when my bank notified me that a substantial deposit had been made into my business checking account and in my email was a signed contract for my services on the Zack Hatter case. I had purposely estimated high, and they had signed off. Like any negotiator, I suddenly wondered if I should have asked for more.

Don't be greedy, I said to myself. Followed quickly by, "Holy crap."

This is actually going to happen.

I sat back in my chair and thought about how I was going to investigate a case in Los Angeles and Mexico from Grosse Pointe, Michigan. How much of it would I be able to do remotely, and how much would I have to do in person? I guessed it would depend on how the investigation progressed. Something told me I wouldn't get too far with my finely sculpted tush in the seat of my office chair in Michigan.

But I would have to play it by ear.

So, in the meantime, first things first.

I typed up a document asking for contact information and numbers of all the people that my client might know. It was a long list with plenty of prompts to get as much information as possible just by filling in some blanks. I emailed that document to Wayne DeGraw. I wasn't sure exactly how often an ex-rock band roadie checked his email, but one could always hope.

Then I sent an email to a friend from high school, Claire Hutchins, who owned a travel agency in Grosse Pointe and asked her to look into flights to Los Angeles and a hotel. I didn't know how much it would cost but I was now working with undoubtedly the largest operating budget of my career. Hell, I could rent a Ferrari if I wanted to. So to say I had quite a bit of wiggle room in terms of traveling expenses was a serious understatement.

And since DeGraw had given me the name and phone number of Hatter's ex-wife, Sunny, I figured that was the best place to start. It would be a little early in Los Angeles since they were three hours behind, but I figured I might as well try.

She answered on the first ring.

After I introduced myself and explained why I was calling, she cut me off. "I can't do this over the phone," she said.

Sunny Hatter cut out any pretense at bullshit.

57

"This isn't going to work," she said. "I need to see your face so I know who I'm talking to."

"Do you want to FaceTime, or Skype?"

"What the hell is that?" she said. "Listen, I'm old school."

"Then how exactly *do* you want to do this?" I asked. I'd had some flaky clients before and I was starting to wonder if Zack Hatter's ex-wife, a woman who went by the name of Sunny, was going to be another on that list.

"I need to see you face-to-face, Mr. Rockne," Sunny told me.

"Call me John, please."

"Okay, John. I know Wayne has vouched for you, based on your work with Clarence Barre, and I was happy to hire you, but starting off like this is too impersonal," she said. "I'm getting a good vibe from you, don't get me wrong, but auras are clearer in person."

Uh-oh.

I sighed. Here I'd told Anna that I wouldn't be jetting off to Los Angeles immediately, but now that's exactly what it looked like I was going to have to do. So Sunny could check out my aura in person.

That sounded so *naughty.*

"Okay, Sunny," I said. "Why don't you give me your address and let me know when a good time for me to visit you in person would be."

Sunny gave me an address in Malibu, which to even a solid Midwesterner like me, rang a few bells. Weren't all the rich people in Los Angeles either in Beverly Hills or Malibu? Didn't Steven Spielberg live in Malibu? I remembered something about a private beach a bunch of billionaires wanted to keep private.

Groovy Train must have done pretty well for Sunny to be living there. Then again, I knew wealthy communities had their fair share of affordable housing. Grosse Pointe was no different. Of course, she had paid my fairly exorbitant fee without batting an eyelash.

She told me she was available most days in the morning, but that she went to a two-hour yoga class every day in the afternoon.

Two hours? What a waste of time.

Clearly, Sunny didn't have a day job.

I told her I would call when my travel arrangements were finalized and we disconnected. I checked my watch and saw that I was almost late for lunch with Nate so I locked the place up and hurried downstairs, out the building, onto Kercheval Avenue in the heart of the Village.

Grosse Pointe was like a small town, really, and its main street was Kercheval Avenue. It was home to several bagel shops, a drug store, Kroger and a few restaurants. There was a giant clock that spanned main street thanks to an elaborate black metal bridge. It looked a little bit like a prop for a Hollywood movie. Main Street, U.S.A.

The downtown saw a fairly high turnover of stores but it had recently stabilized with a home furnishings retailer, anchored by a medical walk-in clinic right next door, just in case the sticker shock caused you to feel faint. Which had been known to happen.

The newest restaurant was a place called Whiskey Six and that's where I'd agreed to buy my friend Nate Becker lunch.

Nate was a lifelong friend and a reporter. He'd worked for the local newspaper, the Grosse Pointe News, before going to the Detroit Free Press, where, unfortunately, he'd been laid off. The newspaper business sucked. After all, who would pay for something they can get for free?

However, as the saying goes, when a door closes a window opens and Nate had thrown himself into the news website business, and business was booming. Online news was kicking its print sibling to hell and back, so if you can't beat 'em, why not join 'em?

His main website was Detroit on Demand, which he described to me as an aggregator with daily articles written by him. But he also had some national websites that dealt with corruption, organized crime, terrorism and all kinds of salacious stories. Nate had always been a prolific writer and essentially launching his own online newspapers had freed his creativity and how he was pumping them out, earning fairly good advertising dollars in the process.

I was happy for him. He'd been through a lot.

I walked into the restaurant, a sleek number with hardwood floors, raised tables and framed photos of old automobiles. I saw Nate in the back of the room and joined him.

"I ordered some appetizers," he said as I sat down.

Nate was a big guy, very overweight, with glasses and a beard starting to show streaks of gray. He was married, with a daughter who had a medical issue and he typically handled stress with food.

Especially if I was buying, which I was today.

"What's the deal with these photos?" I said, looking at the walls. There were pictures of old cars with shady-looking men standing around them.

"Something to do with bootlegging," he answered.

"Ah," I said.

The waitress came and took our order. I got a salad with blackened chicken, Nate a double burger with onion rings.

"So what do I owe this pleasure?" Nate said. "Or are you buying me lunch out of the goodness of your cold, black heart?"

"There's no goodness in my heart, you know that," I said. "Actually, I wanted to talk to you about Mexico."

"Oh, I love Mexican food. If you're going, you have to get the authentic Mole sauce, on chicken. You can't get the real deal here, and it's a pain in the ass to make-"

"Nate, I don't want to talk about Mexican food."

"Oh. Bummer."

I filled him in on Zack Hatter's disappearance and that I was going to Los Angeles to meet his ex-wife, but the last place he was seen was in a place called Bucerias Mexico.

Nate pulled out his phone, tapped at the screen for a while.

"That's not far from Puerto Vallarta," he said. "I know someone in PV." He tapped the screen some more and then my phone dinged.

I looked down and saw that he had forwarded a contact to me.

Roger Goldman.

"He's a writer," Nate explained. "He used to be a reporter but now he writes a newsletter for expat retirees, with a slant toward gay men. PV is home to a huge gay population and Roger is flamboyant, to say the least. Successful, too."

Our food came and we talked about our families, and what he was working on. When it was time to go, I paid and we stepped outside.

Nate put a hand in my shoulder.

"So when do you go?" he asked.

"Probably to LA in a day or two. Not sure if and when I'm going to Mexico."

Nate let out a combination sigh and soft belch.

"Well, be careful," he said. "Mexican prisons are awful and your soft white ass would get ripped apart like a piñata in no time."

13.

"You tell that bitch to go straight to hell," Sunny Hatter barked at Mary over the phone. Mary held the phone away from her ear.

"That kind of attitude runs counter to your name, doesn't it?" she asked Sunny.

"Oh, we got a smart ass, do we?" the woman responded.

Mary debated the wisdom of choosing to start her investigation into the disappearance of Zack Hatter by calling his ex-wife. Mary's client, Connie Hapford, had given her the list of friends and family. The list was very short.

"No ma'am, we have a private investigator here," Mary explained, her voice calm and soothing. "Just trying to find out what may have happened to your ex-husband."

"And you're working for that bitch Connie Hapford? How the hell did she even get my number? You're wasting your time."

"I'm not sure, Sunny," Mary said. "Maybe Zack gave it to her."

Wrong thing to say.

"Bullshit!" Sunny shouted. "That bitch has been trying to steal Zack from me for decades not to mention the fact that she screwed him, probably literally, out of a bunch of his publishing rights. She couldn't give two shits about him. She just wants his money."

Mary sighed. She really hated it when clients only gave her half the truth which happens more than half the time. Mary would have appreciated a little heads up that one of the first names on the list was going to be extremely hostile. It would've been some helpful information.

Mary started to ask another question when she heard a click and then the dial tone.

Great.

Ol' Sunny should have been named Dark Cloud.

Mary dropped her cell phone onto the table with a bang.

"What the hell was that all about?"

Mary looked into her living room where Aunt Alice sat with a glass of Chardonnay. "Another one of your satisfied customers?" Alice said.

The Cooper family prided themselves on sarcasm. And not just any sarcasm, but the nonstop kind. And the more inappropriate time for that humor the better.

Mary still thought back with chagrin to her Uncle Brent's funeral where Kurt decided to make the eulogy into some kind of half-assed comedy routine. Not only was it unfunny, it was extremely uncomfortable. It was the only time in her life she'd actually heard people boo and heckle at a eulogy.

Mary poured herself a glass of wine and joined Alice in the living room. Mary's condo was in Santa Monica and even though it was a block from the beach she had a fairly decent view of the Pacific Ocean. Now, the water was eerily calm, with the occasional jogger trotting past a few tourists taking photos.

"Sometimes my job isn't as much fun as I make it out to be," Mary said.

"Just remember all of the great benefits," Alice said. "Oh, that's right. There aren't any."

Alice had always chided Mary on being a private investigator. Even though she'd solved quite a few cases and had achieved at least a small amount of notoriety and professional esteem in Los Angeles, her aunt felt it wasn't a good career choice.

"Flexible hours," Mary countered.

"Speaking of flexible, did I tell you Sanjay dumped me?" Alice said. "That little pretzel of a man found some big blonde bimbo who does a better downward facing dog than me."

Now a widow of many years, Alice had been seeing a variety of men with a fair amount of regularity. Much more regularly than Mary, in fact, which she occasionally pointed out.

"I guess it's back to Tinder," Alice sighed.

"You're on Tinder?" Mary asked.

"Of course. Aren't you?"

"I am, I just don't use it."

"Well, why the hell not?" Alice asked. "Are you still with Jake?"

Jacob Cornell was a detective with LAPD and Mary had been seeing him off and on for quite some time.

Lately, it was off.

She didn't say anything.

Alice sighed. "What did you say that pissed him off?"

"What makes you think that's what happened?"

Alice laughed. "What else could it be? Oh, wait a minute. Did you cook for him? That would do it, too."

Mary took a sip of her wine.

"Jake's a good guy," Alice continued. "You should do something about him before he comes to his senses."

"Taking dating advice from you is like asking Keith Richards about sobriety," Mary said. "Pointless."

"That's funny," Alice responded, without smiling. "I have to admit that since my hot little Indian pepper Sanjay left I've been in a bad mood. I should have wrapped that little bastard into a Windsor knot and kicked him to the curb."

"Maybe I should call him," Mary said.

"You couldn't handle him," Alice said. Her eyes grew wistful. "For a little guy, he could really jackhammer the daylights out of me."

"Too much information!" Mary said. She stood and went back to her phone.

"Let's hit Tinder," Alice said from the living room.

Mary sighed.

14.

You got a good way to go, a wild way to shine
You got a glass jar in your hand, nose on the line.
                    -Twist One Off (by Groovy Train)

I said goodbye to Anna and the girls the night before I left. The girls acted sad when I said I would be gone for a few days, and it seemed like Anna tried not to act too happy.

But I knew how she was. Probably before the door hit my ass on the way out she'd be on the phone to her book club friends or gourmet group friends or old high school friends or sorority sisters, organizing a night of wine drinking and vulgar humor.

My kind of ladies.

Early the next morning, before anyone was awake, I took a cab to the airport.

I just had a carry-on and my backpack with a laptop ready for Los Angeles. It was an early morning flight, leaving Detroit at around eight in the morning and arriving in Los Angeles around ten. A five-hour flight, minus the three-hour time difference.

Luckily, I had an aisle seat with a skinny hipster in the seat next to me. That gave me a little extra room.

It was too early to sleep on the plane so instead I went over all the notes that Wayne DeGraw had sent me. There wasn't a whole lot to go on. I had also printed off a few articles about Groovy Train and their rise to fame. It was very entertaining reading.

Groovy Train had started after various lineups from different small bands had joined together. They were originally a Midwestern lineup that included a drummer from Akron, a bass player and lead guitarist from Michigan, and a singer from Chicago.

Whether it was simply geographically convenient or not, they began playing gigs mostly in Toledo, with occasional forays into the Detroit area.

Early reviews seemed to state that the group had a nice tight rhythm section and a decent sound but they didn't have any good, original music. It also sounded like their lead singer was drunk at every single show and he had a voice that sounded like a belt sander being used to strip tree bark.

Ultimately, they got a manager who landed them a series of gigs in Los Angeles. So, they left the Midwest and headed for California. Problem was, the lead signer never made it out of Ohio. Instead, he went into rehab and quickly converted to a religious cult, changed his name to Northern Angel and moved to southern Utah.

So when the band got to LA, their manager immediately put a call out for a lead singer. Any lead singer, in fact, as they had gigs booked.

Word eventually came back about a young kid, barely seventeen years old, who had a hell of a voice and was looking for a band to join.

His name was Zack Hatter.

And Groovy Train was on its way.

—

I put away all the documents as the plane began its descent into Los Angeles. I looked out the window, saw the LA skyline with a layer of gray over part of the city. Beyond it, in the distance, I could see the Pacific Ocean.

I'm not gonna lie, a part of me was tremendously excited to work in Los Angeles. I mean, you think of Los Angeles and detectives, you think of Chinatown and Jack Nicholson, Raymond Chandler and The Big Sleep.

Heady stuff, indeed.

The plane landed and I got my luggage, hopped on a shuttle to the rental car area where they had a white Chevy Malibu ready for me.

The irony wasn't lost on me, as my first stop was going to be Malibu. I had debated about trying to go to my hotel first, maybe drop my bags off or if they had a room ready freshening up a bit, but I decided there was no better time than the present.

So I tossed my bags into the trunk, and pointed the Malibu toward Malibu.

15.

When you meet your girl out behind the barn
And tell her that you love her if the truth ain't far
along.
       -Promises (by Groovy Train)

Mary decided to change direction.

She had found that relying on clients for information was a double-edged sword in that the leads were easy to get, obviously, but often they weren't very good. And just as often they hid the truth. Half the time, the most important contacts were the ones clients didn't want her to have.

So based on the feeling that Connie Hapford might not be the most transparent of employers, Mary made the decision to reach out to Sly Witherspoon. Sly was a legend in the Los Angeles music scene. A former studio musician turned engineer turned producer turned manager.

He agreed to meet her at a guitar store where one of his clients was autographing instruments for fans.

The store was called Skull Tronic and when Mary parked, she had to find a spot several blocks down from the store due to the line that meandered out into the street.

Mary had never heard of the Skull Tronic music store, but judging by the people in line, it probably didn't cater to her musical tastes.

She bypassed the line and went into the store, saw a guy with a huge head of black hair scribbling away on people's guitars with a black Sharpie, and finally spotted Sly, standing over by the keyboards display talking to a young woman in a leopard skin skirt and high heels.

Mary didn't want to cockblock him so she hovered nearby until Sly spotted her. Mary watched the young girl give her phone number to Sly who keyed it into his phone and then he came over to Mary.

"Kind of young, isn't she?" Mary asked. "Is she out on recess?"

"She said she was nineteen," Sly answered. "I'm taking her at her word."

Sly was like Keith Richards without the charisma. Oh, he had a little style, but he looked mostly like what he was; a washed-up rocker still hanging on to the music scene. Cool enough to attract young women, but not talented enough to make it big. Still, she kind of liked Sly. He made no apologies for what he was.

Mary had gotten to know him when an alcoholic bass player had sued Sly and his management company for injuries from a concert at a state fair. The guy claimed he'd fallen off the stage because he'd slipped on cow manure that was stuck to his boot.

It had been fairly easy to get proof that the injury was fake, especially when the bass player drank a fifth of whiskey while surfing at Zuma Beach.

Cow manure, indeed.

"So who's the big star over there?" Mary asked, nodding her head toward the black-haired guy signing guitars.

"Name's Stevie Saturn. A real douche."

"He's your client?"

"Yep. He and his band. Death Hole."

"That's the name of the band? Death Hole?"

"Yep."

"Wow, that's great marketing. And he's a douche?"

"A mega douche," Sly said. "Dude has a little bit of talent but a monster ego, along with a monster addiction to coke and booze. Horrible combination."

Mary looked around.

"Is there a better place we can talk?"

Sly glanced toward the back of the store. "Sure, let's go over to the guitar room."

He led her to a little room set up as a place to test guitars, but no one was playing so the room was empty. They stepped inside and Sly shut the door.

"So what can I do for you?"

"Zack Hatter has gone missing," Mary said. "And I've been hired to try to find him."

Sly started laughing. "Why?"

"Why what?"

"Why does anyone want to find him? He'll fucking show up in a couple of weeks, looking like hell and broke, maybe even beat up a little bit. It's what he does." He narrowed his eyes at Mary. "Are you actually looking for him or are you just taking a paycheck?"

Mary rolled her eyes. "Of course I'm taking a paycheck. What, do you think I work for free?"

"No, I meant–"

"I know what you meant," Mary said. "Don't get your panties in a bunch. To answer your question, yes, I'm actually looking for him. He's been missing for longer than usual, plus, no one's been able to find anyone who's seen him since he disappeared in Mexico a few weeks ago."

"Mexico? That's not a good place to disappear," Sly pointed out, stating the obvious. "Those narcos will cut your balls off and stuff 'em up your nose."

"Who's got balls that will fit in their nose?" Mary asked. She nodded her head toward Steve Saturn. "The douche?"

"It's just an expression," Sly answered. "Seriously, though, you've always got to be careful in Mexico. Even those sleepy little fishing towns the tourists love to discover. They've got narco watchers."

Mary could see she needed to be more direct. "Okay, look. Do you know of anyone who might know where he is or how to get in contact with him?"

Sly looked up at the ceiling.

"Where in Mexico was he?"

It was her turn to pause. The name eventually came to her.

"Bucerias," she said.

"Ah! Sure, he was probably down there seeing Bulldog."

"Bulldog?"

"Yeah, he's this fat white guy from the Valley. He made a shit ton of money bootlegging porn," Sly explained. "He disappeared down to Mexico and has a place in Puerto Vallarta, which is just south of Bucerias, I think, where a bunch of rock guys go to party. He's paid off all the local cops and federales down there. I guess it's a hoot. He's got local strippers and hookers, booze, pot, coke, heroin, meth. Anything you want, from what I hear. But he doesn't really deal. Because of the fucking narcos."

"Yeah, you told me about the narcos."

They could see the table where the douche was signing guitars and he suddenly stood up, looked around, then waved at Sly.

"Oh, great," Sly growled. "Looks like I gotta go."

"Hey, does Bulldog have a real name?"

"Sure," Sly said. He looked at Mary.

"What is it?"

"I don't know. But I'm sure he's got one." He smiled and Mary laughed in spite of herself.

"Look," Sly said, "Puerto Vallarta is actually a pretty small town once you get to know it. I've been there quite a few times." His eyes grew wistful. "There was this hot peasant girl-"

Mary cut him off. "The douche is getting antsy."

"Okay," Sly said, hurriedly. "If you go there and ask around for Bulldog, you'll be able to find him, no problem. But stay away from the narcos. A pretty little thing like you. Boy, they would kill for you, chica."

Mary winked at him.

"So what you're saying is they have excellent taste."

16.

Show me a memory filled with hate and rage
Tell me a tale, the kind not fit for stage.
                    -Tequila Nights (by Groovy Train)

The famed Pacific Coast Highway did not disappoint. The Pacific was a calm sheet of blue steel and I saw a few surfers on the sand, waiting for the wind and waves to pick up.

This was the Los Angeles I'd seen in the movies.

I turned on the radio, hoping to catch a Beach Boys song but all I could find was pop and alternative music so I turned it off. Secretly I'd hoped for some sweet karma and that a Groovy Train song would just so happen to be on the radio, proof that my taking the case was some kind of cosmic sign.

Instead, all I got was Whitesnake.

Eventually, the road climbed slightly and I turned into the bluffs of Malibu. I was half expecting some kind of gate or something where you would only be let in if you drove a super expensive import. Or maybe you would have to show your mobile banking account and that it had a six-figure balance, at least.

75

But there was no gate, no weird entrance. Just a winding road that led me past increasingly big and expensive-looking houses.

Sunny Hatter's house was fairly modest, in my opinion. I was thinking of some Malibu mansion you see in helicopter shots from the opening credits of a television show. The kind with sprawling grounds, maybe a few horses, and a Rolls-Royce parked in the huge, winding driveway.

Not to mention, there are some fairly large estates in Grosse Pointe, so I was surprised to pull up in front of a low-slung ranch house that had clearly been built in the seventies. It was long and low, painted white with light blue window shutters. There was a Spanish-style terra cotta roof and a mature yard filled with tall oak trees.

I parked the rental car in the driveway and walked up to the house, shocked there wasn't a gate.

But like any community, Malibu probably had a pecking order and despite the fair amount of money Sunny most likely had, she couldn't afford the high-rent part of Malibu, even though the low-rent was not affordable to even modest millionaires.

The door opened and a woman in yoga pants and a black T-shirt opened the door.

"Mr. Rockne?" she asked.

"Yes, please call me John."

She stuck out a hand. "I'm Sunny. Please come in."

Sunny was a beautiful woman, no doubt about that. Light hair, stunning blue eyes and a yoga-type body. She was definitely a mature woman, but the kind at first glance you would assume was in her thirties, not her fifties.

She had on a cotton peasant blouse that hung down and I couldn't tell what she had on underneath, if anything. Her legs were long, tan and muscular. I caught the faint scent of a subtle perfume that made me suddenly feel relaxed. Or maybe it was Sunny's vibe. See? Southern California was already rubbing off on me.

I followed her inside.

While the exterior of the house wasn't much, it proved to be highly deceptive because the inside was spectacular. It was huge, with big rooms and at the rear of the house, I saw a spectacular swimming pool with a cabana and an outdoor seating area with a fireplace.

The furnishings inside were all modern, clean and bright.

It was a stunning house.

"Do you mind if we sit outside?" she asked.

"Not at all," I said. "I was stuck on a plane for five hours, some fresh air would be great."

We took a seat at the outdoor dining table and I heard music in the background. Definitely not Groovy Train. It sounded like mystical music from India that made me feel even more relaxed. I realized there was a possibility that if I got any more relaxed, I might fall asleep.

There was an array of potted plants around the seating area and I saw an iguana on top of the stone wall. He was enjoying the sun. He seemed very relaxed, too.

"First of all, thank you for taking the case," she said. She smiled, revealing a row of perfect white teeth.

"Thank you for hiring me," I said. "It will be a challenging case but I like a challenge."

"Challenging how?" she asked.

I chose my words carefully. "Whenever anyone disappears in a foreign country, there are always complications. Nothing that can't be handled, but it does add a layer of complexity."

"Not to mention the other private investigator." She raised a light, perfectly arched eyebrow at me. Her skin crinkled just a little bit, another indication she was older than she looked, but it was the kind of imperfection that made her look even more attractive.

I looked at her as the gist of what she said landed and I felt a tickle of anxiety. "What other private investigator?" I asked.

She shrugged her shoulders. "I don't know. Some bitch. She called me before you did, asking questions. None of which I answered." The word didn't sound as harsh as it might have, probably because of the setting. But it was still a little jarring.

I let that one go, for now. But I didn't like the sound of it. Another private investigator could make things super complicated. I would have to get more information on that unfortunate development.

"Did she say who she was working for?"

"Nope, but then again, I didn't ask."

I decided to set the issue aside for now. "So what do you think happened to Zack?" I asked. Standard operating procedure. Hear what the client thinks and later, use it to compare what you've found.

"I have no idea, really," she said. "I just know him better than any other human being on this Earth and something happened. It could be really bad. Or just really unusual. In any event, something happened and I thought I could wait it out, but I can't. Not with my conscience remaining intact. It has been leaving me out of balance, my healer even said so."

"Okay," I said. "What about where he went? Or the purpose of his trip in Mexico?"

Sunny sighed. "Supposedly there is a friend of his in Puerto Vallarta where Zack would sometimes go to stock up on some of his pharmaceuticals. From there, it's anyone's guess. I've heard the names of a few small towns around PV, but I can't say for sure."

"Do you know the name of this friend?"

"I don't know a name, just a nickname."

She looked at me and the blue in her eyes was amplified even more from the reflection of the pool. In them, I could see real emotion. Say what you will, I got the distinct impression this woman cared deeply about Zack Hatter.

"Bulldog," she finally said. "They call him Bulldog."

17.

She got the kinda skin that just belong
On a sheet made of silk
And a hand that do no wrong.
  -MiniSkirts & Major Trouble (by Groovy Train)

Mary felt naked without her gun. It was a .45 Para-Ordnance high-capacity semi-automatic. Fully loaded, it was a hell of a gun and had saved Mary's bacon more than a few times. But now, she took it out of her shoulder holster and placed it inside her gun safe along with the ammo and a spare clip. There was no good way to travel internationally with a gun. She could try to take it officially and show her private investigator paperwork, but it all depended on which official you were lucky, or unlucky enough, to get, and if you wanted to waste multiple hours at the airport.

In the end, she knew that it was incredibly easy to get a gun in Mexico. Not necessarily a high-quality weapon, but if push came to shove she could become armed.

But, for now, she was going to go without.

Mary checked her watch. Ordinarily, the amount of time she had would be plenty good to make it to the airport. But you never knew with Los Angeles traffic. She could be sitting on the 101 long enough to get her AARP card.

The clothes in her closet definitely needed updating but she figured the weather in Mexico wouldn't be all that different from Los Angeles. Maybe a little more humid. So she picked a variety of stuff betting on mostly warm weather, along with some rain gear and a couple of items if it got too cool.

She decided to call Aunt Alice to see if the woman could take care of the plants in her condo. It was kind of a pointless idea, though, because the last time she'd asked everything had died. It was hard to tell if they'd been overwatered or simply nagged to death.

"I'm coming with you," Alice said, after Mary told her she was going to Mexico for a case.

"No, you're not," Mary responded. "I'm working. This isn't a vacation."

"First of all," Alice said, "quit trying to make it sound like you're some kind of serious professional because we both know that's a line of bunk."

"Bunk?"

"Plus, even if you do have to run around and ask a few people some silly questions, we both know you'll be back at the hotel pool ordering margaritas and trying to get a cabana boy to oil up your backside."

Jesus, Mary thought.

Although, she had to admit, that did sound kind of nice. And there was at least some small amount of truth in what Alice was saying.

"You're just going to get in my way," Mary said. "Plus, it could be fairly dangerous, between my case and Mexico itself. You know, narco terrorists, gangs."

Alice cackled. "Dangerous? Honey, my middle name is Dangerous."

"I thought it was Gretchen."

"Gretchen or Dangerous, I forget," Alice said. "It doesn't matter. I'm coming with you. I haven't been on a trip out of the country since I went to Canada for cheap Viagra for Walter."

"Who's Walter?"

"Oh, honey. Walter was a love machine. Until his ticker gave out. We were doing reverse cowboy and I felt him go stiff. You know, his body, not his-"

"Enough!" Mary chastised herself for not being quicker to cut off her aunt when she got too graphic. Which was pretty much all the time.

"When is our flight?" Alice asked, not missing a beat.

On the one hand, she knew it was a terrible idea. On the other hand, she knew Alice spent a lot of time in her house, alone. Especially since yoga instructor sex god Sanjay had taken off.

Knowing it was a mistake, Mary gave her the information and they agreed to share a cab to LAX.

She finished packing and rolled her suitcase out to the front door.

Next, she went into her office and packed up her small laptop, power cords for both the computer and her cellphone and some notepads and pens.

Next, her passport and plenty of cash, also from the gun safe.

Mary's last stop was to her bathroom. She hunted through various drawers and shelves until she found a small bottle of Pepto-Bismol and some leftover antibiotics. She made a mental note to remind herself not to even brush her teeth with tap water. She'd heard it could be that bad.

Finally, she was good to go. She used her Uber app to order a car, first to pick up Alice and within a half hour her phone buzzed to tell her that her ride was ready.

She locked the condo, went downstairs and saw a guy with a minivan waiting at the curb.

He got out and popped the rear door and Mary hoisted her bag inside. She kept her backpack with the laptop and her identification with her.

Mary slid into the middle seat and Alice patted her on the shoulder.

"Hola, Gringa," she said.

Mary rolled her eyes.

Alice held up a miniature paperback whose cover stated it was a collection of Spanish expressions.

"You better learn some of these," Alice said. "You know, like 'please don't hurt me' and 'help.'"

Mary ignored her but for the bulk of the ride to the airport Alice read aloud a variety of expressions that she felt would be useful for both of them.

-Kiss me there.
-More lime, less salt.
-Let yourself out in the morning.
-My groin hurts.
-Nice ass, sailor boy.

Mercifully, they finally pulled up at the departures area and they got their bags and went inside. They found the place to print off their boarding passes and once they had them, they turned toward the security line.

"Hey, wait for us!" A voice that sounded sickeningly familiar to Mary shouted at her.

She turned and saw Uncle Kurt and her cousin Jason hurrying toward them.

Mary looked at Alice who suddenly had a sheepish expression on her face.

"You've got to be fucking kidding me," Mary said. "You told them we were going to Mexico? You *invited* them?"

"Watch your mouth," Alice snapped. "And yes, I did. I felt bad, but it just kind of slipped out."

Kurt and Jason stopped in front of them and Kurt high-fived Alice. "This is going to be a friggin' riot," Jason said. "I've always wanted to do some gigs in Mexico. Then I can call myself an international sensation!"

"How are you paying for this?" Mary said. "Because I'm not footing the bill."

"Jeez, what do you think I am, some kind of goddamn leech?" Kurt said. "Hell no. Jason here hit it big with Algae, they've got a number one song!"

Mary and Alice both looked at Jason, their faces registering no small amount of skepticism.

But Jason shook his head.

"No hits," he said. "Other than our tour bus. Someone ran into us and each of us got two grand if we promised not to go to the cops."

"You've always got your music," Mary said.

"Get it?" Kurt said. "A big hit?"

He looked from Mary to Alice, who simply looked back at him.

"Christ, I hope the audiences are friendlier in Mexico."

"Don't count on it," Alice said.

Mary turned and began walking to the security line.

Mexico.

With Alice, Kurt and Jason.

Suddenly, the thought of a Mexican prison didn't seem so bad.

18.

Take me down to Rio
Where the girls love me hard
Take me down to Austin
I'll play my final card.
           -Wicked Nylon (by Groovy Train)

There was no doubt in my mind I was going to have a date with Bulldog in Mexico. Which sounded like a really bad idea or a movie starring Sandra Bullock.

But I weighed my options.

Zack's last known whereabouts was Mexico. Specifically, the Puerto Vallarta area. I could spend more time in Los Angeles gathering background, but time is of the essence in missing persons cases and the trail might already be cold. If I waited any longer, it would just get colder. Maybe even downright frigid.

I checked my phone and saw that my former high school friend and current travel agent, Claire Hutchins, had put me on a flight to Puerto Vallarta and booked me into a hotel there, too, per my request. I had plenty of time to get to LAX but I am chronically early to airports. So I turned the rental car for the airport and put my Bluetooth device around my ear and voice dialed the number for Zack Hatter's son, Ringo. Sunny had told me about the kids she and Zack had, then went an extra step and gave me their contact information. Since Ringo lived in Oregon, I figured any information he might have would be limited, but I had time so I figured I might as well make use of it.

"Hello?" the voice on the other end of line asked. It was a great voice. Deep, just a little bit of an edge to it. The son of a singer, of course.

"Is this Ringo Hatter?"

"Yea."

"My name is John Rockne and I've been hired by your mother–"

"Don't know where he is, don't give a shit," Ringo said, cutting me off.

To the point, I liked that.

"Wait, your mother said you live in Oregon?"

It was a quick question to stop him from hanging up on me, which is what it sounded like he was about to do.

It worked.

"Yep, Portland," Ringo said. "It's far enough away from all the LA bullshit." He sighed. "Listen, I work for a living. Do you need something from me?"

"Just wanted to know if you've heard from your…Zack."

He laughed softly. "I haven't heard from that deadbeat in years. What's wrong, is everyone worried he finally OD'd?"

I thought I detected a hint of caring in the question, even though he phrased it to sound like he didn't care.

"More like people just don't know where he is," I said. It was hard to tell if Ringo was actually this cynical and jaded, or if he was trying too hard.

"Don't know. Don't care," he said. "Anything else?"

"Not that I can think of."

"You're not going to call my sister, are you?" he asked.

"Um…" It was the next call on my list but I didn't want to admit it. Bette Hatter. A math professor in Seattle according to my notes.

"Please don't. We've put up with all of this shit all of our fucking lives," Ringo said. "People finding out who we are, wanting interviews, or stories or memorabilia hunters. And every time it happens, we get pissed off at having to be reminded of our absentee father."

I narrowly avoided a school bus that suddenly veered in front of me on the freeway. Why was a school bus on the freeway, and why was its driver acting like a NASCAR fan?

Only in LA.

"Believe me, you'll get the exact same answers from her that you just got from me," Ringo continued. "With maybe a few more expletives."

"OK, well, I'm on my way to the airport. I'm flying to Mexico to see if I can track Zack down. I'm sure you won't think of anything, but if you do, please feel free to call me at this number."

"You're right, I'm sure I won't think of anything. Be careful in Mexico, though. A buddy of mine just got back from there. He was stung by a scorpion and picked up herpes. Not from the scorpion. At least, I hope not.

"On that note," I said. "Thanks for chatting with me."

We disconnected and I immediately voice dialed the number for Bette Hatter. I figured Ringo was telling the truth, but the stone unturned was sometimes hiding the key.

The stone unturned. I like that.

If I found Zack, I would give him that line as the start of a song idea. I would make millions.

Bette Hatter answered, and Ringo was right. She reiterated a startling lack of desire to discuss the father she hardly knew. And tossed in a few curse words.

The call ended just as I pulled into the rental car return lot. I grabbed my bag and made it to the departure area via a shuttle bus. Inside, I printed off my boarding pass, breezed through security and arrived at my gate with nearly an hour to spare.

I took a seat and thought about calling Anna to let her know I was about to fly to Mexico. I got out my phone and started to call her.

A scent tickled my nose and I recognized the unmistakable presence of marijuana. I glanced at the young man a few seats away from me. He had long hair, was lanky, and sported a T-shirt with what I guessed was a band name on the front.

Algae.

19.

Playgrounds and booby traps
Trippin' on the hour.
She aint' been over here
Since that mornin' shower.
                    -Jill (by Groovy Train)

Rutger arrived in New York rested and ready thanks to the business class ticket provided by his employer. Clearly, this was going to be a big job, but he already knew that as double his normal fee had been guaranteed.

He wasn't in the least bit fatigued from the long flight. He'd flown business class, stretched out in a lounge seat, thoroughly satisfied by what he'd done both professionally and personally in Bangkok. If someone had indeed once said it was a bad idea to mix business and pleasure, well, that person was a moron. Rutger had thoroughly enjoyed taking out the Canadian, and then having his way with the girl.

Now, back in the United States, Rutger felt a mixture of comfort and boredom. He liked traveling overseas and while it was good to be back, he already missed the sense of adventure. Oh, well. He knew that boredom wouldn't last.

This was going to be a big job.

He caught a cab to a nondescript cinder block building in Brooklyn. Its front door was glass, coated with black film to prevent prying eyes. The steel frame looked extra sturdy.

Rutger pushed the recessed button to the right of the door and waited. Above him, he heard an electronic pulse as the security camera looked him over.

The door buzzed, he opened it and stepped inside.

The biggest Asian man Rutger had ever seen stood before him. He had exotic tattoos around his neck and face, but in the dim light Rutger couldn't make out what they were.

With a nod of his giant, square ahead, the man indicated he wanted Rutger to lift his arms for a search.

Rutger complied.

He wasn't the least bit intimidated by the size and demeanor of the giant in front of him. In his experience, the adage that the bigger they are the harder they fall was certainly true. Guys like this had rarely been tested. Their skills were minimal and usually quite rusty.

But Rutger showed none of this as the man searched him.

Satisfied, the Asian hulk turned and led Rutger into a large space divided into several rooms by colorful silk screens and dark wood frames.

The music overhead was an acoustic guitar, bluesy, seeming in stark contrast to the décor.

Eventually, they arrived in the middle of the labyrinth where there was a large, open area and an Asian man wearing dark slacks, a billowy white shirt and a fedora hat. His hair was combed straight back, but with a little wave like the start of a pompadour. His small black eyes were set close together and his narrow, wide mouth looked like a crease in his face.

In his hands was a guitar and Rutger realized the music wasn't coming from a sound system, but from the instrument in the man's hands.

They stopped, and Rutger heard the giant leave behind him and the partition was slid shut.

The guitar player in front of him finished his playing with a flourish and set the guitar in its stand.

He looked up at Rutger and smiled, revealing brown, crooked teeth. They looked like opium teeth, Rutger thought.

"It's a 1930 Martin OM-45 Deluxe," the man said. His voice was heavily accented, singsongy, underscored with a strange penchant for inconsistent volume.

"Very, very rare," the man continued. "Only six of them were ever made. I own three of them, hmm?"

Rutger wasn't sure if the 'hmm' was an actual question or a verbal tic.

"Do you play all of them at once?" Rutger asked.

The man smiled at him, but no humor showed on his face.

"I've made a fortune getting what I want in life, Mr. Rutger," he said. "What is that expression Americans love? 'Where there's a will, there's a way?' So true, hmm!"

Vocal tic, Rutger decided. Since it seemed like the man wasn't going to give him his name, he decided to call him Mr. Hmm.

"In the right hands, a great guitar is like a surgical instrument," Mr. Hmm said. "Precise. Crystalline. Of course, not all musicians are capable of realizing its true potential. For those, anything will do because they may as well be banging their hands on a bongo, hmm."

He giggled, revealing even more crooked buck teeth.

"My associate, the large fellow who showed you in? He is effective, but not overly precise. The project I'm giving to you requires deftness of touch, hmm?"

Rutger nodded.

"There is a man who either has, or knows where, a certain item is located. I need you to find that man and hold him for me so that I can question him in person. I do not need him killed right away. But after I have what I want, then you may kill him. But only then."

That was not the kind of job Rutger enjoyed.

"Not exactly my specialty," Rutger answered. "I'm known for eliminating problems. Not babysitting them."

Another high-pitched giggle. "Babysitter! Hmm! That's why I've doubled your fee, Mr. Rutger."

The door behind him slid open and a woman appeared, also Asian, dressed in a slim black suit. She had a slim leather folio and handed it to Rutger.

"You'll find everything you need in there," Mr. Hmm said. "Your best bet is to start in Puerto Vallarta, Mexico. Travel has been arranged. Once you have found him, there are instructions in your folio for how to contact me. Until then, there will be no communication between us, hmm."

Mr. Hmm picked up his guitar and began plucking at the strings.

Rutger turned and walked out. As he did, the melody of the song playing triggered something in his mind. He recognized the tune. Who was it by?

It took him a moment, but he remembered the name of the band.

Groovy Train.

20.

Don't tell me that you love me when your face is full of lies.
Don't tell me that you love me when your face is full of lies.
I'll take you out behind the Caddy and feed you to the spies.

    -Morning Glory Blues (by Groovy Train)

I buckled in and tried to relax. The flight would be a short one, a little more than two hours and I planned to spend most of the time playing chess on the new app I'd installed on my phone. It was great. You could play a game and then afterward the app would analyze your play. It seemed to be especially fond of counting my "blunders," which was an actual term the game analysis provided. Humiliating, but there you go.

When the app was done examining my poor play, I got out my notes on the Hatter case and read through them again. Unlike most of my cases where the subjects were fairly ordinary, Zack Hatter's background made for highly entertaining reading. I soon found myself reading for pleasure, especially about the legendary brawl in an after-hours bar in Paris. Zack had ended up being secretly driven across the border into Spain as authorities in France wanted to arrest him.

My life suddenly seemed super boring

"Do you go to Mexico often?" a voice to my left asked me. I had gotten the window seat, as requested, and I had barely noticed who was sitting next to me. Now, I turned.

It was an older woman, with a pleasant, attractive face. She was smiling at me and I immediately liked the mischievous twinkle in her eye.

"No, first time," I said.

"So you're a Mexican virgin?"

I raised an eyebrow at her but I could tell she was having fun with me.

"I guess you could say that," I replied.

"Me too," she said. "Looks like we'll be losing our virginity together."

This time I outright laughed. This woman was flirting with me, I was fairly sure. I was kind of flattered, too. She was an attractive woman for her age, and back in the day I imagined she'd been a hottie.

"Whenever I imagined losing my Mexican virginity, I always pictured it being with someone just like you," I said. Hey, I can flirt with the best of 'em.

"Oh my!" she said, her face turning a slight tinge of red. I smiled inwardly. So she wasn't *that* good at flirting. I took a secret pleasure in out-flirting her.

I stuck out my hand. "John Rockne," I said.

She shook it, a nice firm handshake that lingered a bit. "Alice Cooper," she said. "Not the rock star."

"Too bad, I could've been one of your groupies," I said.

She laughed again and looked at me. "I'm starting to like you," she said. "What are you doing in Mexico?"

"Plastics," I said.

"Like in The Graduate?" Alice said. "Wasn't that a line from the movie? 'Plastics. There's a great future in plastics. Think about it.'"

"You're right," I replied. "Great movie."

"Yes," Alice said. "There's a lot to be said for that older woman, younger man dynamic. Very sexy."

I think I actually blushed at that one.

"So what, do you sell plastic?" she asked.

"Sort of," I replied. "I represent a company who supplies different kinds of plastic to the automotive industry. There's a lot of plastic in cars these days."

"Cars and Beverly Hills housewives," Alice said.

"True," I replied. "What are you going to Mexico for?"

"Vacation. I'm a professional masseuse back in Los Angeles. Where are you staying in Mexico? I'd love to get you on the table. First session is on the house."

Holy cow. This woman was something else.

"Um, I'm not sure," I said, then felt bad when I saw her reaction. She thought I was lying. I dug through my briefcase/backpack and found my itinerary.

"Casa Pacifica," I said. "It's a Marriott Hotel, I guess. How about you?"

"I think it's the Westin," she said. "Downtown."

"Oh, I'm downtown, too. If we bump into each other, I'll buy you a margarita."

She patted my hand and let hers linger on mine for a moment.

—

96

"That sounds like a plan, John. And remember," she said knowingly, making direct eye contact.

"What happens in Mexico, stays in Mexico."

She then actually winked at me.

21.

The spirit of a man ain't too hard to tell
Show him the door to heaven
Then kick him down to hell.
　　　　　　-Cracker Man (by Groovy Train)

Mary found Alice waiting for her after deboarding the plane. Kurt and Jason were sitting even further back than Mary. Mary had been sitting behind Alice.

"Jesus Christ, why didn't you just rip your clothes off and throw yourself at the poor man?" Mary said. She'd overheard Alice's flirtatious conversation with the man in the seat next to her. Mary had felt a mixture of embarrassment and appreciation for the show. It had been more entertaining than the in-flight movie.

Alice shrugged her shoulders. "We had a nice conversation," she said. "There was definitely a spark. I can't help it if my natural pheromones send out a signal and men come knocking. Happens all the time."

"It wasn't your pheromones, my dear," Mary said. "It was your mouth that never knows when to stay quiet. Didn't I tell you I was on a case? To lay low? Don't make a scene?"

"'Lay' being the operative word here," Alice said, smirking at Mary. "Besides, you sound kind of jealous. Did you see what a hottie this John is?"

"I'm not sure I would call him a hottie," Mary said. She had watched him stand up after they'd landed, out of curiosity after hearing the salacious conversation. "He's kind of cute in a domesticated, suburban way."

"Well, I think you're jealous."

"I'm not jealous," Mary said. "I'm working. You need to remember that."

Kurt and Jason finally caught up with them.

Kurt stretched out his arms. "Fucking A that flight sucked!" A few people in the terminal turned and looked at him.

Mary wondered why she'd even bothered to scold Alice. There was no way this group was ever going to lay low. They were a traveling circus.

"Someone was dropping ass the whole time," Jason muttered.

"That was me," Kurt said. "I had a ton of bean dip last night in preparation for the trip," he said with a voice chock full of pride. "Sorry, but I had to let loose. That kind of trapped gas is dangerous." He seemed to reconsider that idea, though. "Then again, the pilot said we had a nice tailwind that got us here sooner," Kurt added. "That was no tailwind. That was my ass."

"Too much information, Kurt," Alice said.

"Is that really true?" Jason asked.

"Who says Americans aren't classy?" Mary said. "Come on, let's go through Customs and get our stuff."

It took them two hours to get through it all, but eventually, they found their way downtown to the hotel. The ride had been uneventful, the four of them packed into a creaking minivan. They'd passed a lot of old cars, people on ancient motorcycles without helmets. Occasionally they'd gotten glimpses of the Pacific and on the horizon, glimpses of the mountains.

The hotel was, in fact, a Westin. And it was downtown. Mary and Alice were sharing a room. Their window looked out toward the ocean.

"Great view," Alice said.

"Yeah, it's a nice place for you to get away from your day job of being a masseuse, right?" Mary said. She still couldn't believe Alice had uttered that whopper.

"That's not really a lie," Alice said. "My massages are so good, people think I'm a pro. John won't know the difference." She cracked her knuckles.

"Why don't you go get us a drink downstairs while I get some work done?" Mary said.

"You read my mind," Alice said. She left the room and Mary took the opportunity to set up her laptop on the hotel desk, connect to the Wi-Fi and check her messages. Nothing urgent.

What was urgent was finding Bulldog, and hopefully getting a solid lead on the whereabouts of Mr. Zack Hatter. The Mad Hatter. All Sly had told her was that if she asked around Puerto Vallarta, she was bound to find someone who knew where Bulldog lived, or at least where he hung out and how to find him. Sly had implied that Bulldog wasn't very good at keeping a low profile. Something he shared in common with Mary's current entourage.

Mary fired up her Internet browser and searched venues for live rock music in Puerto Vallarta. There were several shows tonight, all clustered around the downtown area.

Perfect.

She could hit all of them and ask around, hopefully get a lead on Bulldog.

But first, she was going to go down to the bar and join Alice.

See what all this fuss about Mexican tequila was about.

22.

Came into New York with a belly full of blues
Coasted into Denver with a mouth full of fumes.
        -Smoke 'em Out (by Groovy Train)

From one high-rise to the next.

Rutger liked the new digs.

Mr. Hmm's assistant had booked him into a private penthouse condo with scads of room and a balcony that ran the entire length of the place. The inside was painted a mixture of beach-themed pastels, seafoam green being the color used most liberally.

Everywhere were reminders he was in a tropical beach paradise. Ceiling fans featuring blades that looked like palm leaves, seashells embedded into the tile floors, and artwork featuring depictions of colorful ocean fish.

It suited Rutger very much.

His operating budget for this job was indeed quite large and he wasn't surprised his accommodations were so luxurious. But even if the client pushed back which Rutger knew he wouldn't do, he would take care of the cost himself out of his fee. For double his ordinary charge, it would be more than enough to cover this extravagance.

And Rutger liked to go first class all the way.

There was a knock at the door and Rutger spoke out loud to himself. "Must be the hooker."

Still, he brought his pistol out from behind his waistband and held it as he took a quick peek through the peephole. Never a good idea to take a lingering look through it, in case an assassin like him had his muzzle directly against the peephole and was waiting for the light to change and shoot.

Rutger himself had killed people using that very method, on more than one occasion.

He approached the door from the side, careful to not let his shadow show under the doorframe. He also took care to not make any noise in case the person on the other side was waiting for some sign that the room's occupant was standing right in front of them.

Rutger had waited outside a hotel room many a time, waiting for the slightest noise or change in light to tell him his quarry was on the other side of the door.

He opened the door to a stunning Mexican beauty with no tattoos per his request. Rutger stepped back and put the gun behind him underneath his shirt and inside his waistband.

No need to terrify her from the very beginning. That could come later.

She walked in and Rutger looked at her ass as she went past him.

Very nice.

She had a small handbag which he was positive had a gun inside along with some dope.

Almost immediately after checking into the condo, he had ordered some female companionship. A lengthy tryst upon landing in a foreign country always helped settle him, helped his focus.

This time, he had requested a 420 friendly from the escort service. 420 was slang for pot and Rutger hoped she had brought it and that it was snuggled up against the pistol in her bag. He would retrieve both at the same time.

She did a slight turn in the room and Rutger noted it was performed with the express intent of giving him a nice view of her body and to make sure he approved of the merchandise before any activity began.

He did.

The merchandise was quite splendid.

"Why don't you hop in the shower?" Rutger nodded his head toward the bathroom.

He hated dirty hookers. Which is why he always ordered the top shelf escorts. He was rarely disappointed. And if one had the nerve to show up at Rutger's hotel room less than clean, well, she would pay the price, not him.

The hooker took her little bag with her into the bathroom and Rutger heard the door lock.

Which was fine because it allowed him to take his gun and put it near in the night table's drawer next to the Bible.

She could theoretically come out with her gun and try to rob him as was done quite often with the gringos in Mexico. But Rutger was confident that he could get the gun away from her and break her neck without too much trouble. She had laid a big joint on the table with a lighter per his request so he fired it up and took a deep hit.

The cost of the marijuana would be added to his final bill and he was sure that a 200% markup would occur. But he just smiled and took a deep lungful of marijuana. Having the prostitute bring the drugs was better than him going out onto the street and trying to score some. The idea of getting busted for some pissant pot buy and missing a contract like this one would be a disaster.

He took another hit from the joint and felt its acrid taste work its way down his throat and into his lungs.

He generally avoided drugs. Certainly the hard stuff when he was working but nothing wrong with a little toke now and then.

Rutger checked his phone and reread the message from his employer with the address of Bulldog's apartment. Apparently ol' Bulldog was having a big party that night at his swanky digs in the ritzy part of Puerto Vallarta.

With his ample amount of cash on hand Rutger figured it would be no problem to crash the fiesta, especially if he brought along this hot little hooker to help him gain access to the party without any problems. Men trying to get into a party alone sometimes could be difficult even when hefty cash bribes were offered. But beautiful women were always welcome, and this one was quite spectacular.

She must have read his mind because just then the door to the bathroom opened and she stood there in all her glory. Black stockings, garters, black bra and a big smile. Her long black hair flowed down her shoulders and Rutger noticed she was clean-shaven all over.

He put down the phone, stood up, pointed to the floor and began to unbuckle his pants.

His instructions to the hooker were brief and to the point.

"Get on your knees."

23.

Bleedin' like an angel
Cryin' like a liar
Flyin' like a lion
Dyin' on the fire.
                 -Hotel Yucatan (by Groovy Train)

My hotel room was nice albeit modest. I had certainly stayed in worse places than the Casa Pacifica.

At the same time, it wasn't a mega-fancy resort hotel with sweeping views of the ocean. In fact, my view consisted of the ugly-ass end of another building.

But that was fine. I wasn't here to sightsee. I was here to find The Mad Fricking Hatter.

I actually felt sluggish after the flight and the idea of a nap crossed my mind but I quickly ruled it out. Caffeine would be a better solution. Besides, I didn't want to start off my investigation in Mexico by snoozing. That's not exactly what my clients were paying me to do.

So I set up shop in my room. I hung up my clothes, got my electronics organized, which meant chargers and laptop power cords hooked up and running.

I also made a mental note to exchange some of my American dollars for pesos. I had programmed Roger Goldman's cell phone contact information into my phone. He was the writer for newsletters catering to the gay community about how to vacation in Mexico and more specifically Puerto Vallarta. His name had been given to me by my friend Nate back in Grosse Pointe.

I punched in the numbers and waited. After about the seventh ring a voice answered.

"Hello?"

"Hi, is this Roger?" I asked.

"Yes sir, how can I help you?"

Roger Goldman had a great radio voice. Smooth and very cultured.

"Nate Becker is a friend of mine and he recommended I contact you," I explained. "I'm a private investigator looking into the disappearance of someone here in Puerto Vallarta."

"A lotta people disappear here," he pointed out. "How is Nate, by the way?"

"Nate is hungry," I said.

Roger laughed. "I hope he's taking care of himself, though. He's a good guy. Smart. Talented. Hate to see him go too young."

I had thought the same thing many times, but Nate had told me to back off, so I had.

"Well, Nate is Nate and no one is going to tell him otherwise," I pointed out.

"That's the guy I remember," Roger said. "So how can I help you?"

"Well, I'm looking for someone and apparently the trail is going to run through someone called Bulldog. A music–"

"Yep, I know him. Has a place on the ocean. A penthouse. I was there once a few years back, but I can't say I remember much about it. Everyone knows someone who knows him, though. He's kind of a legend around here."

"Do you have an address or a phone number for him?"

Roger laughed. "No, that's a well-kept secret here in PV. His parties are highly exclusive, everyone wants to go because he has a lot of celebrities, most of them music-related but some not. Justin Bieber was down here awhile back."

"The Bieber?"

"Indeed. Lamborghinis racing up and down the streets all hours of the night. Look," Roger paused. "Do you have cash? An expense account? You said you're a private investigator, right?"

"Yes to the private investigator question, no to the cash question."

"Shoot. You could always go to a club and throw enough money around, you might get invited to one of Bulldog's parties."

"Even if I had some cash, it probably wouldn't be enough."

"Tell you what," Roger said. "Since you're a friend of Nate's, I might be able to help. I have a friend of a friend of a friend who has some connections to the music biz down here. He might be able to get you an invite. Let me make some calls and pull in some favors."

"I appreciate it," I said. "I'll do what I can to compensate you for your time."

"Don't worry about it."

We disconnected and I let out a sigh. I really didn't want to put all of my eggs in Roger's basket. Oh, that sounded a little weird. I didn't want to rely only on Roger's good faith to get me in to see Bulldog. There had to be another way.

Maybe I would find it in the bar.

24.

I wanna hear you say
Wanna hear you say
Wanna see you pay
For every yesterday.
          -No, No, Not Today (by Groovy Train)

Mary changed her mind. When she saw Alice, Kurt and Jason sitting at the hotel bar, she sneaked past them and out the door. She was here to work. Besides, if she stopped and had a drink with them, they would probably want to come along. And that was definitely *not* going to happen.

Even more accurately, Mary knew all about Mexican tequila from a not-so-distant wild youth.

Now, she stepped out onto the sidewalk and debated about whether to drive, but one of the clubs was only a few blocks away so she figured she would get some exercise while she was at it. So she struck out on foot, feeling the power of the Mexican sun on her shoulders.

The air was humid and the sun seemed to get hotter with each block she walked. This wasn't southern California sun. This was the real deal.

Mary didn't speak Spanish, so the street names started to blend together. Calle this. Calle that. Eventually, she found her way to a club called The Hot Rooster.

Hmm, she thought. Lots of ways to have fun with that one.

There was a cover charge of one hundred and fifty pesos, which Mary paid and went inside. The music, which hadn't been terribly audible outside the club, immediately announced itself with a thumping bass line and some horrible guitar noises.

Oh God, Mary thought. *It was going to be like Algae all over again.*

She half expected to see Jason up on the stage, bellowing one expletive after the other.

Luckily, it wasn't Jason, but a group of young locals doing their best to imitate some kind of rock/punk band from New York during the early nineties. Mary went to the bar and ordered a mojito. She didn't really like tequila, even the expensive stuff. There was no doubt it was smooth, but the flavor didn't do much for her. Besides, rum sounded good to her.

"Hello there."

Mary turned and came face-to-face with the bare chest of a very tall man. She glanced up, and saw a scary-looking face. It was dark, with dark eyes, and horrible teeth. Short black hair was cut in an even bang across the man's massive forehead.

He looks like a Mexican Frankenstein, Mary thought.

"Hola," Mary said, barely getting the word out of her mouth. What she really wanted to say was *holy shit*.

"How do you like Puerto Vallarta?" the giant said, his voice sounded like a garbage truck. With a missing muffler. "I can tell you're not from around here."

"You're both enormous and perceptive," Mary pointed out. "I like it fine, so far. But the parties are lame. I'm from LA and am used to killer parties. With celebrities, especially musicians."

Sasquatch let out a long laugh. His breath smelled like barbecued meat.

"You are in the wrong place," he said.

"You mean PV?"

"No, this place. Nothing good happens here. Except for me meeting you."

The human Sequoia smiled, revealing a mouth full of teeth, each the size of an apartment-sized refrigerator.

"Oh yeah?" Mary asked. "Where's the action?"

"Let me show you," he said. He held out a hand that resembled a catcher's mitt. Mary let him walk her to the door.

"Hold on," she said. She chugged her mojito and set the empty glass on the bar. It gave her a chance to consider what she was doing. This club looked like a dead end, but then again, the giant might have a car waiting on the curb to kidnap her.

In the end, she decided to be adventurous.

"Let's do this," she said. Mary let the giant lead her out of the club, around the corner, and into another club, this one called La Boca Grande.

It was full of locals, at least they looked like locals to Mary, and the music was a great kind of Latin groove, almost a boogaloo.

Now she had to figure out how to ditch Lurch. "Going to el bane," she said. The giant nodded his melon-sized head and Mary disappeared into the crowd. It was a throng on the dance floor, groups of people dancing alone and together, some smoking cigars, holding drinks, doing the cha cha or the salsa, whatever it was.

She did, in fact, use the restroom. It was a squalid place, the stench nearly burning her nostrils, but Mary did her business and then rejoined the throng in the club. She was thirsty so she bought herself another drink and was about to duck back into the crowd when a stunning-looking woman grabbed her by the arm.

"Girl, what are you doing here?" the woman asked. "You've got LA written all over you!"

The speaker was a woman, with the kind of harsh beauty that's unforgettable. Dark, smoky eyes, hatchet-sharp cheekbones, lips to die for, and a knockout body. She wore a little black dress showing off her perfect legs. *Damn*, Mary thought. *And she's perceptive. How did she know I'm from LA?*

"And you've got hotness written all over you," Mary said. "Do you–"

"Get away from her," the voice boomed from behind Mary. She didn't even have to turn to realize it was her giant escort.

For a moment, Mary thought he was telling her to get away from this beautiful woman. But then she realized it was the other way around.

"Fuck off, Brody," the beautiful woman said.

"Go to hell, Tara," the giant said.

At least now Mary had names to put to the two angry faces squaring off.

The giant grabbed Mary and started to pull her toward him.

Suddenly, Tara had a butterfly knife in her hand and made a move toward Brody, the giant.

"Whoa!" the overgrown pituitary gland said.

He let go of Mary.

"You want a piece of us?" Tara hissed. She danced forward with stunning speed and power, slashing at Brody, who stumbled backwards and fell on his ass. It was an enormous crash, like a steer carcass being cut down at the slaughterhouse.

Tara held out her hand to Mary. "Let's get out of here."

The two of them left the club and found themselves out on the street.

"Wow," Mary said. "You sure know how to show a girl a good time. The next thing you'll tell me is you're a friend of Bulldog's."

Tara laughed and looked at Mary with a quizzical expression. "How'd you know that?"

"How'd you know I was from LA?"

Tara laughed. "Good point. Hey, Bulldog's having a party tomorrow night. Want to be my date?"

Mary smiled.

"I thought you'd never ask."

25.

This is how it's gonna be
You and me
This is how it's gonna be
Now I see.
                    -Right As Rain (by Groovy Train)

Roger Goldman was a good lead, but I needed more. It was too early to hit the clubs, and I needed some time to think about my next step. Plus, I had some time before I was meeting Roger at a bar a few blocks away.

The best place to wait?

A pool.

Or a bar.

Or a pool with a bar.

The hotel had a swim-up bar, the kind where the shallow end of the pool was a bar, with stools half-in and half-out of the water. I was not wearing a swimming suit and so I had no intention of partaking in alcoholic beverages while half-submerged, although the idea was enticing. And maybe, after a few drinks, I would find the idea more attractive.

Then again, I was here to work, not to vacation.

So instead, I went to the "dry" side of the bar, sat down and ordered a Pacifico beer.

"There's my gringo!"

A little head popped up, barely over the edge of the bar from the swim-up side and I saw the woman from the airplane. I smiled in spite of myself, and tried to remember her name.

"Alice," I said. "How are you?"

"Great," she said. "How's the plastics business, John?"

"Booming," I said. "Buy you a drink?"

"Of course," she said. She slid onto one of the poolside bar stools, across from me.

"I'll take a margarita, senor," she said to the bartender.

I sipped from my beer while the bartender made her drink. When he finally slid it over in front of her we toasted each other.

"To Mexico," I said.

"And whatever happens," she replied.

I laughed. Again with the flirting.

"I thought you were staying at a Westin?"

"I am," she said. "But they have a bar and pool reciprocity with this hotel. The Westin doesn't have a swim-up bar. Plus, I heard all the hot guys hang out here."

"How's the water?" I asked, not quite sure what to think of Alice.

"Invigorating. You should join me. Go skinny dipping, I won't tell." Alice smiled and took a big slug of her margarita.

"I would love to," I said. "I am a firm believer in the buddy system."

"I'll be your buddy, John."

I laughed. "And I'm sure you'd be a great one."

The beer felt good, and I thought about Zack Hatter and Bulldog. It seemed incongruous that the aged rock star was being held captive here in PV. Sitting at a hotel swim-up bar probably had something to do with that emotion.

Alice and I chatted through one more beer and another margarita, until I felt guilty about not working the case.

"I'm afraid I have to run to a meeting," I said to her. "About plastics. So I'll take a rain check on the skinny dip."

"Okay, John," she said. "If you ever want to check out the Westin, feel free to stop by. I'm in room 408."

The rest of my beer went down with a few easy swallows and then I settled with the bartender.

"Ok, maybe I will. I'll see you around, Alice."

"Hook up with you later, John." She followed that with a double wink.

Outside, the air felt a little cooler than near the pool deck, and the breeze was more noticeable. Roger, Nate's writer friend, had given me the name and address of a bar where he would introduce me to someone who might know Bulldog. He'd also hinted that if I had at least a little bribe money, that I could possibly make it happen.

The place was called El Gringo Barracho. The drunken gringo. Perfect. After the two beers at the hotel, I wasn't drunk. But I had laid a decent foundation.

It took me less than five minutes to find the place. There was no cover so I walked inside. I noticed two things right away. One, the scent of cologne was overpowering. And two, the place was full of men.

I checked my watch. It seemed early for a club to be this packed, but hey, when in Mexico, right?

Right after that, realizations number three and four followed. Three, it was a gay bar. And four, the dance floor was packed. They were all standing in the middle, as if they were waiting for something.

A hand waved to me and I saw Roger sitting at a table with an extremely overweight man with pasty white skin and bright red hair. He had freckles all over his face and the world's thinnest goatee.

There was an empty seat at their table so I sat down.

"Hey Roger," I said. I had looked up his newsletter website and there had been a photo of him, a headshot, which made recognizing him easy. He must have done some homework on me, too, because he'd picked me out of the crowd.

"John, this is Gustavo," Roger said. "Gustavo, this is my friend John I was telling you about."

We shook hands and I was about to ask a question when shouting from the dance floor erupted. I turned, and saw that high above the dancers, suspended from the ceiling, was a giant foam machine. Bubbly foam began to pour down on the dancers below in great quantities. The men ripped off their shirts and began dancing and rubbing foam all over each other's bodies.

John, you're not in Kansas anymore.

I turned back to Roger and Gustavo, but both of them were eagerly transfixed on the action behind me. A waiter appeared and I ordered a Pacifico over the din.

Mercifully, the suds dispenser finally stopped and both Roger and Gustavo suddenly seemed to realize that I was sitting across from them.

"Sorry, what were you saying?" Roger asked me.

I looked at Gustavo. "It's very important to me that I get a chance to talk with a man named Bulldog. Do you know him? I heard the only way to meet him is to get invited to one of his parties."

The pasty man nodded his carrot-topped head. "Are you rich?"

"No, I hail from middle-class suburbia."

"Are you connected to the music industry in some important way?" The red-haired ghost had a high-pitched whiny voice. His hand snaked out from underneath the table and snatched up his drink. Something with a mint leaf in it, in a clear plastic cup.

"I love music, but I don't do anything to help create it," I admitted.

Gustavo turned to look at Roger, as if to say, why am I here listening to this loser.

"I believe John is willing to offer a finder's fee to the person who can get him a personal invite to Bulldog's. How much that might be is between the two of you."

Stifling the urge to cringe, I reached into my pocket and took almost all of my petty cash, a little over a grand. I whipped it out and said, "I've got a grand if you can get me in. Once I'm in, I might be able to get a little more."

I dropped the cash on the table.

Gustavo had a smirk on his face. There was no way he was going to agree to the fee. That much was obvious.

Roger leaned over and whispered something in Gustavo's ear. The pasty mound of flesh softened his expression, raised an eyebrow at me, and swept the money off the top of the table.

"Give me your cell phone number," Gustavo said. "And be ready. I'll text you an address and a time for tomorrow night. Wear something that will make it look like you actually belong at a party, please not what you're wearing now." He looked me up and down with open disdain. "You look like a first-grade school teacher on a field trip.

Gustavo got up and left the table, leaving behind an aura of contempt, and a sickly sweet scent of body odor.

"Thank you, Roger," I said. "I could tell he wasn't impressed with my financial contribution. What did you say to him to get him to accept?"

"That if he gave you what you wanted, I'd give him what he wanted," Roger said, with a sly smile. His teeth were perfect. "And Gustavo wants him."

Roger lifted his chin toward the dance floor. One man was alone on the dance floor, nearly naked, spinning and gyrating, rubbing his hands over his suds-covered body.

I nodded.

"Well," I said, "cleanliness *is* next to godliness."

26.

The blood of a renegade boiling in the sun
The soul of a musician drowning in my rum.
                    -Natchez Trace (by Groovy Train)

Rutger felt good.

He almost killed the hooker, but decided not to. Puerto Vallarta wasn't his home base by any means, and he'd never really worked in the city before. Disposing of a body wouldn't be impossible, but it would add a lot of work to his plate.

In his line of work, simplicity was always the best route.

So while he was admittedly a little rough on her, okay, a lot rough on her, he let her live. Instead of killing her, he gave her a huge tip, a grand, and sent her on her way. Physically, she wouldn't be able to work for a few days. The bruises, scratches, and internal damage would take time to heal and she would lose wages for a while, so the tip seemed fair.

Rutger felt well rested as he'd slept most of the afternoon, like a lion who'd feasted on a fresh kill.

Now, he went down to the hotel's gym and pumped iron for an hour, followed by an hour-long burst of cardio that left him drenched with sweat. His work was usually more about precision than outright physical conflict, but it was important to him to stay in top condition, just in case.

Rutger ordered a light meal from room service, and then changed into a dark silk suit, his only accessory being a forty thousand dollar Audemars Piguet watch. He had the invite in his pocket to the party hosted by Bulldog welcoming New York rapper Lucifer T to Puerto Vallarta. His employer in New York had some connections with the music industry and had provided the link, rendering the need for a beautiful girl to help him get into the party moot.

He packed up his few items, left the room and tossed everything into his rental car.

Rutger wasn't planning on coming back.

He decided to walk, rather than taking a cab, to the address he'd been given by New York. It belonged to a high-rise on the beach, clearly brand new and upscale, but not necessarily the biggest building in PV.

Still, it reeked of money and exclusivity.

There was a bar across the street with an outdoor seating area and Rutger went there, ordered a club soda with a lime, and watched the building. The sun had already disappeared below the horizon but enough ambient light provided a good viewpoint for Rutger. He was curious who would show up and when.

For several hours, Rutger watched the building with interest. Occasionally, he got up and walked around, changed tables, even went to a nearby coffee shop and watched from their outdoor area.

Mostly, he was looking for anything out of the ordinary. He'd survived in this business because he was extremely good with a gun. That was first and foremost. It wasn't the Old West, but some of the worst scrapes of his life had come down to who could get their gun out the fastest and then who was the most accurate.

Rutger had never lost.

After that, he owed his existence to a passion for caution. He was careful in everything he did. Rutger often imagined it as if he had a movie projector in his mind and he had the ability to run an action through the projector and watch how the movie played out. The hooker he decided not to kill, for instance. The film got bogged down when it came to the part about getting rid of the knockout body.

So he mostly watched now for any sign of an ambush. Maybe his employer in New York wanted to double cross him. Use him as a setup to scare a customer. Or to draw out a rival criminal element. It could be anything.

What always caught his eye was the presence of a weapon. He knew exactly what to look for. Most of the time there was never any discernible shape underneath a man's jacket, or inside a woman's waistband. It was more about the way someone moved when they were armed. It was always different. And often times it came down to intuition, just knowing that someone was carrying a gun, even when one wasn't visible.

As some of the early arrivals made their way to Bulldog's building, he spotted several people carrying. Most of them, he assumed, would be working security. He could tell by their clothing and presence that they were low-rent.

No, what would really catch his eye was a top tier professional.

And so far, Rutger knew he was the only one present.

Finally, the time came for him to make his appearance. It was still early by party standards, but he hadn't seen any entourage arrive so Rutger figured Bulldog was already on the premises. Probably via a private elevator, or maybe the party was in his personal apartment, although Rutger doubted it.

Figuring that Bulldog was onsite was all Rutger needed to set his operation in motion.

He walked into the lobby of the building, found the elevator where two security guards waited for him to present his invitation, which he did.

The two men were careless and clearly expected no trouble. They had their hands at their sides and when one looked at Rutger's invite, the other made no move, which showed how clueless he was.

With a nod of his head the security guard gestured for Rutger to enter the elevator. He pressed the button for the penthouse and waited. It was a fast elevator and it whisked him to the top in no time. The doors opened and he immediately heard the music, smelled the unmistakable dance-club odor: men's cologne and women's perfume, marijuana, cigarette smoke and booze.

There was a hallway that led to some oversized double doors in front of which stood two more security guards, a matching pair to the ones downstairs. Rutger again showed his invite and again, they carelessly waved him inside.

The doors opened and he stepped into the giant room. The floor was a clear sheet of quartz, dangerously slippery but spectacular, especially since it wore the reflection of the enormous picture windows at the other end of the room that were filled with the brilliant photo-like image of the Pacific Ocean. The illusion was that the floor felt like the sky and you were floating over the ocean.

Quite impressive.

A scantily clad server with a tray of champagne appeared in front of Rutger and he accepted a glass. The room wasn't crowded, as it was still early, but he could see other various rooms, some of them looking like temporary creations, like private booths at a club.

Rutger sipped and began to prowl the place looking for Bulldog.

He wasn't here to party.

He was here to do his job.

27.

I like to roll 'em in the mornin'
And smoke 'em through the day
I love to pound their wicked thighs
When they beg my boy to stay.
                    -Fat Girl Blues (by Groovy Train)

Mary met Tara for a pre-party drink, just down from Bulldog's apartment. She'd pretty much wasted the day, doing fruitless research on the Mad Hatter, looking for the most recent photos of him. She'd scoured the local music clubs, guitar shops, drug dealers and prostitutes.

No one had seen Zack Hatter.

She even took a break and popped into an Internet café and armed with a triple espresso, had used some of her back door Internet tools supplied by a hacker friend and former client.

Zilch.

The odds of her actually seeing him on the street, or at the party, were infinitesimal, of course, but she looked for the most recent photos of him, preferably candid shots taken by snoopy fans. The professional shots, used for publicity, made him look ten or twenty years younger.

The place Tara had suggested was a martini bar, and Mary found her new friend halfway through a drink and she was flanked on each side by men who seemed very interested in her attention.

"Please, make room for my friend, Mary," Tara urged the man to her left. He slid down one and Mary took his place.

"I'll take a dirty martini," Mary said to the bartender, after she'd exchanged a hug with Tara, and marveled inwardly at how firm the woman's body was. *She must spend a lot of time in the gym*, Mary thought.

"How are you tonight, chica?" Tara asked her.

"Ready for a party," Mary said. "Un fiesta grande."

Tara laughed, exposing a beautiful row of perfectly white teeth.

"Then you have come to the right place. Tell me, what kind of man are you looking for?" she asked. The men on either side pretended as if they hadn't heard the question. " I can tell you need one," Tara continued. "Or your vajayjay needs one who can really take it for a pounding."

Mary felt herself blush just slightly. "I have very high standards when it comes to men," she said. "They have to be able to walk and chew gum at the same time."

"We have a few of those, not many," Tara said. "Come, finish your drink and let's go to a real party."

Mary tossed down her martini and they walked a few blocks down the street and after showing the security guards Tara's invite, they walked into Bulldog's apartment.

"Not bad," Mary said. The place would fit in just fine in Los Angeles. It looked swanky. "Maybe I'll get a place like this. Right after I become an Internet billionaire."

Tara snatched a couple glasses of champagne from a passing server and they strolled their way through the crowd, literally rubbing shoulders with Puerto Vallarta's music celebrities.

"So what does Bulldog look like?" Mary asked. As much fun as she was having, she was here to work. And she wanted to get in close to Bulldog before things got really crazy and he became impossible to find. This apartment would hold a lot of people and Mary figured they would really start flowing in once the clock struck midnight.

"He used to be pretty hot-looking, but he may have been getting paid in tamales," Tara said. "He's packed on the pounds recently. Think of Andy Garcia wearing a fat suit."

Mary pondered that for a moment. "Okay, got it," she said.

Suddenly, much to her surprise, she saw someone she recognized. At least, thought she recognized.

It was the decent-looking man Alice had practically thrown herself at on the airplane ride down here. He was standing with a guy, very overweight, with skin so translucent it looked like he was glowing.

Mary took the opportunity to step away from Tara and she walked up to the two men. The one she recognized glanced at her and Mary knew he recognized her, too.

"Where's your date? The old lady from the plane?" Mary asked him.

He looked oddly at her, caught off guard.

She stuck out her hand. "Mary Cooper. You sat by my aunt on the plane ride down from LA. I was sitting behind you two and heard her sales pitch. Are you two going to get married down here?"

He relaxed, smiled and shook her hand. Mary liked the look of him. Slightly above average-looking, in relatively good shape. But she liked his face, which had a quiet intelligence and a hint of a smart-ass.

"John Rockne," he said. "No, we're not getting married. Since I've already got a wife back in the US, I think I'm going to have my way with her and then toss her aside when vacation's over."

Said with a straight face, Mary wasn't sure if he was joking or not, but then a little smirk started at the corner of his mouth.

Yes, Mary thought. *One of my kind.*

"Well, be sure to wear protection," Mary said. "She's got more crabs than Red Lobster."

"Well, I had planned to sample the seafood down here, but now I'll think twice," Rockne said. "What are you doing here? Vacation? Work?"

"I'm a tuna wrangler," Mary said. "All the sushi here in PV? It's from me."

The big white man standing next to Rockne took that as his cue to move on from the conversation, departing with a look of distaste on his face.

"Interesting," Rockne said. "You don't look like a fisherman. Or fisherperson. What kind of boat do you have?"

"I don't use a boat," Mary said. "I spearfish. I swim out and bam! Shoot 'em through the head with a spear gun. It's more sporting that way."

"I would imagine."

"So what do you do, when you're not attending hip parties down here?"

"Plastics," Rockne said. "I live in Detroit and supply plastics to a lot of different companies involved in the auto industry. It's very exciting. Puts your story of spearfishing for tuna to shame. Aren't you embarrassed?"

"Yeah, sort of," Mary said. "I–"

Before she could finish her sentence, a scream erupted from somewhere in the apartment, followed by multiple gunshots.

Mary reached for her gun but remembered she didn't have one, and Rockne put his arm around her and together, they ducked down, but instead of joining the crowd, they both went instinctively toward the gunfire.

28.

*You've never seen the wind or tasted whispered love
Until you've been up to the clouds and rained down
From up above.*

*-Lost in Mountain Grove (by Groovy
Train)*

Despite his strict adherence to a patient approach, Rutger simply had no time for this.

A bunch of obnoxious posers.

They walked around like they were geniuses. Pretending to be great artists creating important works that would be timeless.

Yeah, right.

In reality, most of what they were making was ghetto crap purchased mostly by suburban white kids who wanted to be considered gangsters. Or insipid pop tracks whose sole goal was to get into somebody's head and stick there, like a bad advertising jingle.

The only people of redeeming quality were the women. There were a lot of beautiful women who, unfortunately, Rutger had to ignore for now.

He was here to work.

He could tell there was an etiquette involved, in terms of getting the opportunity to speak with Bulldog. It was like the man was holding court and small groups of people waited in the wings for when it was their chance to find a lull in the conversation and then dive in. It was practically like a wedding where people line up to congratulate the people involved.

Rutger wasn't about to wait.

He strolled up to Bulldog, interrupting some black guy with a gold chain and a goofy hat.

"I've got a message from some mutual friends in New York," Rutger said. He didn't smile, didn't offer an apology for interrupting. He communicated the severity of his message by the delivery.

The small group was silent. A bodyguard pushed off from the wall and started to stroll over.

Rutger smiled as the man approached.

The tough guy rapper immediately turned tail and disappeared. The bodyguard stopped in mid-stride as Bulldog waved him away with an *I can handle this* kind of expression.

"No. You can't," Rutger said quietly.

"What?" Bulldog asked.

Rutger looked at the man before him. He had once been slim, maybe even athletic. But now he carried the extra weight of a jock gone to seed. He had expensive clothes and had fine features. Dark eyes and lashes that were almost pretty, like a woman's.

"Where is Zack Hatter?" Rutger asked.

"How the fuck should I know?"

Rutger took his silenced automatic out from the holster inside his suit jacket and shot Bulldog in the left elbow. The gun spat, like a loud cough, but it was mostly disguised by the loud music.

Bulldog yelped and grabbed his arm.

Rutger pushed him toward the back of the room and its floor-to-ceiling windows.

"Once more," he said quietly to Bulldog. The bodyguard behind him was frozen, too. Cheap security, they were the worst. "Where is Zack Hatter?"

"Jesus. You shot me."

"No, my name isn't Jesus, but you can pray to me if you want. And yes, I shot you." He tilted the gun up and shot Bulldog in the right elbow. "Now I've shot you again."

Another scream but this time Bulldog couldn't grab his elbow since his other arm was shattered as well.

"He's in Bucerias," Bulldog gasped. "Zeta! Jesus Fuck!"

Los Zetas? Rutger thought.

Those were some bad dudes. He'd subcontracted a local Zetas gang in Los Angeles to do some dirty work for him years ago.

They were horrible people.

Worse, they were unprofessional.

Rutger nodded, unscrewed the silencer from his pistol, glanced at the windows behind him. He pointed the gun and fired a series of shots at the window in a rough circle and then grabbed Bulldog and threw him through the weakened section of glass.

The room erupted in screams from the booming gunfire and crashing glass and Rutger jacked a fresh clip into his automatic, turned and fired above the heads of the security guards who had finally mustered enough courage to start to approach him, but by now were being swallowed by the crowd.

The massive panicked and fleeing herd of wannabes were Rutger's friends, though, and he slipped comfortably inside it as the mass moved toward the exit.

29.

Spinning out my mind and shaking all you free.
I wonder what she did and if she thought of me.
          -Taken Street (by Groovy Train)

I hadn't been to very many parties in Puerto Vallarta; okay, this was my first one.

Ever.

But I instantly had the feeling that the shooting had something to do with the disappearance of Zack Hatter. I don't know why. And the thought came into my head and then it was gone again.

Instinctively, I put my arm around the woman I'd just met, Mary Cooper. She slipped out of it just as fast and I saw her reach for her waistband and I expected her to come out with a gun but her hand was empty. I knew her story about being a tuna fisherman was bullshit, and now I wondered if she was a cop. Or a drug enforcement agent of some kind.

But I set that issue aside and pushed forward, toward the sound of the gunshots. If Zack Hatter was here, it was my job to get him.

Horrified faces rushed past me. Drinks were spilled.

I saw a woman running with one high-heeled spiked shoe on, and the other foot bare. A guy raced past us carrying a bottle of champagne in one hand and his car keys in the other.

"Let's find Bulldog," Mary said.

I glanced at her out of the corner of my eye.

She wanted to talk to Bulldog, too? Why?

"Up here," I said. There was a short set of stairs that seemed to lead to a private seating area that looked down upon the sunken pool outside. But from here, I could get a quick respite from the flood of people pouring out from the back of the apartment.

Finally, the flow slowed and Mary jumped back into the river of people, plowing her way forward.

I followed her and we soon came to an expansive seating area surrounded by several gigantic television screens, a DJ booth and various sets of leather couches.

One of the huge picture windows had a man-sized hole in it and a few security people were standing by it, looking outside.

I walked up by them and looked out, too.

Way down on the ground I could see a man splayed out. A small crowd had gathered around him.

"Let's go," Mary said.

We joined the crowd and followed it down the stairwell, out onto the pool deck where the body was.

On the ground was a husky man, wearing a white suit, the front of which had several large holes surrounded by blood. His hair was slicked back and he had a vaguely handsome face, although it was now misshapen from the fall.

He reminded me of a chubby Andy Garcia, the actor.

Except that he was clearly dead.

"Who the fuck are you?"

I turned and it was one of the security guards, red-faced and angry, probably feeling fairly inept. Apparently he hadn't guarded Bulldog's security very successfully.

"We're DEA," Mary said, before I could respond. *DEA?* I liked it, and it made sense why she went for her gun. But if she was DEA, why didn't she have it on her?

"We need to know what happened here," she said.

"What's it look like?" he barked at her. "Some asshole shot Bulldog. Tried to make him talk. Then threw him out the window."

"Talk about what?"

"How the fuck would I know?"

"It was something about being fatter in Bucerias," a voice said to my right. It was another security guard, but this one didn't have an attitude and it looked like he didn't have an appetite for blood. He looked like he was about to toss his cookies.

"Fatter in Bucerias?" I asked.

Both security guards and Mary ignored me and continued to look at Bulldog's body.

"Are you sure he didn't say Hatter?" Mary asked. "As in Zack Hatter?"

"As in Zack Hatter is in Bucerias," I said.

"Con Zetas," the shocked security guard said.

"Shut your mouth," tough guy security said. He was glaring at the guy who'd just spilled his guts because his boss's guts had been spilled first.

"With Zeta? Catherin Zeta-Jones? Married to Michael Douglas?" I asked.

Mary looked at me. "Los Zetas. The gang."

"Oh, yeah," I replied. "I've heard of them."

Sirens started blaring and Mary looked at me again.

"Let's get out of here before we end up in a Mexican prison. You'd be the flavor of the day. Every day," she added.

30.

Move on down the line
Move on down the line
Jump from car to car
But don't go back in time.
          -Regretting Train (by Groovy Train)

Mary wanted to head back to the hotel, pack up and head to Bucerias, but first she had to confront John, if that was even his real name.

"Okay. Who the hell are you and what are you really doing here?" Mary said.

They had left the scene of Bulldog's demise and were walking in the general direction of Mary's hotel. She had no idea where he was staying, or for that matter where he lived. Maybe he lived here year-round.

John looked at her with a bemused expression on his face.

"I told you, I'm in plastics," he said. "For the automotive industry."

"And I'm the lead ballerina at the Bolshoi."

"You are? That's cool. I didn't know you were Russian. You do have a dancer's body, though."

"Why don't you take your plastics story and–"

He stopped looking at her and the playful expression on his face vanished.

"I've got a better idea," he said. "Why don't you tell me who you really are? One minute you're the world's best-looking tuna fisherman, the next you're with the Drug Enforcement Agency. I'm not sure I believe either one."

Good-looking?

"I'm a helluva fisherman," Mary said.

"Do most tuna wranglers carry a gun?" John asked. "When the commotion broke out, I saw you reach for your sidearm out of habit. Seemed like a pretty practiced move to me."

"Well aren't you just a little nosy Rosie?" Mary countered.

"And you're clearly not with the DEA otherwise you'd have a car, and a radio and a partner of some sort," he retorted. "You wouldn't be freelancing with some guy you just met on the plane."

What the hell, Mary thought. "Okay, here's the deal. I'm a private investigator from Los Angeles looking into the disappearance of Zack Hatter. Now, quid pro quo, Clarice."

She saw the puzzled expression on John's face.

"You never saw Silence of the Lambs?" she asked.

"Oh, I get it. That's right. Quid pro quo. Okay, screw the plastics story."

Mary paused and raised an eyebrow. "Okay, this is going to be good."

"What a coincidence," he said with an easy smile. "I'm a private investigator from Grosse Pointe, Michigan looking into the disappearance of Zack Hatter."

Mary shook her head. "How in the hell did a private investigator from Michigan get assigned to the case of a missing singer from Los Angeles? Are you doing some kind of long-distance marketing I should know about?"

"I wish," he replied. "No marketing. The truth is, it's a long story, let's just say that I had a previous case involving a musician and that person had a connection with Zack."

"Obviously, two different clients," Mary said.

John sighed. "Now that you asked, though," he said. "How about you? How did you get tied up with this case? Obviously you're in LA so you must know people in the music business. "

"Excellent deduction," she said. "You really are a good detective."

John laughed.

"Yeah, I consider sarcasm a lost art," she said. "Some people fail to see its value. True sarcasm must be defended at all costs."

"That's great, but you still didn't answer my question," John pointed out.

A city bus wheeled around the corner, went wide and jumped the curb in front of them before correcting and careening back into the street.

"A former client referred me to the new client, which is how I get about 99.9% of my business," Mary said as they continued walking. "I considered plastering Hollywood with billboards featuring my face but figured I would only get calls from movie producers."

John nodded. "I tried coffee cups once," he said. "But after a couple of rounds in a dishwasher the ink wore off."

Mary realized they were in front of her hotel.

"Okay, how are we going to do this?" she asked.

"Seems to me like it would make sense to work together," John said. "And I don't think it would be unethical to our clients because if we solve the case faster they'll come out ahead in terms of money. So it's perfectly logical to me."

"If you promise not to slow me down, I'll let you be my assistant and we can meet in Bucerias," Mary said with a straight face.

John's face took on a serious look as he contemplated the notion.

"I've got some people I'm traveling with," Mary added. "You might remember my horny aunt. Alice. It sounds like a kind of insect. The Horny Ant. Anyway, I have to go back and we'll check out of the hotel."

"Okay, I agree to *you* being *my* assistant," John said, "as long as you don't get in my way. I have to check out, too, and then I'll head up to Bucerias. Let's meet either late today or tomorrow morning and figure out a strategy for finding Zack or the Zetas."

They exchanged cell phone numbers.

"Let's shoot for Zack and try to avoid the Zetas," Mary said. "Mexican gangs aren't good for a gringo's health."

"All right," John said. "And try not to get into any trouble between here and Bucerias. I don't want to have to save your life again."

Mary put her hand on his shoulder.

"Yeah, you avoid trouble, too," she said. "I can't always be around to bail you out."

31.

It's gone and you know and it won't come back.
It went to hell when you fell off the track.
                -Straw Dog (by Groovy Train)

Mary walked in the hotel room and saw Alice and Jason standing over Kurt who was sprawled on the couch slathered in some kind of white cream. He had a wet, rolled-up towel across his face.

"What the hell is wrong with him?" Mary asked. "He try some comedy on the beach?"

"He's doing his best impression of a lobster," Alice said. "The big dumbass went down to the beach, drank too much cheap beer and fell asleep and then got scorched by the sun."

"Please Merciful Mother of Jesus take me into your blessed arms!" Kurt wailed.

"Come on Dad. Toughen up man," Jason said. He was sitting in a chair across from the couch. Mary had thought he was asleep.

Kurt tried to sit up but then fell back onto the couch. "You go straight to hell, Jason! God damn, you should've woken me up!"

"I fell asleep too," Jason said. Then he added with a touch of snark. *"In the shade."*

Mary was surprised. She had never heard Jason speak so coherently. Maybe the Mexican air was waking up his brain.

"Come on, pack your shit up. We're leaving," Mary said to the group. She still couldn't believe Bulldog had been shot and tossed out a window. Maybe there was more money at stake than she'd been led to believe.

No matter what the truth was, getting out of Puerto Vallarta as soon as possible was a good idea. She had a feeling the Mexican authorities wouldn't be knocking on her door anytime soon, considering how many hundreds of people had been at the party. But still, why wait around to find out?

"We can't leave," Alice snapped at her. "I met a hottie. Remember the stud on the plane? And I need to have my way with him before we leave. Several times," Alice said. "I just need another hour with him and maybe a drink or two to get him into my web."

"That sounds gross, Aunt Alice," Jason said.

"Shut up, Jason," Alice replied.

Mary sighed. Sometimes it was tough being a Cooper.

"I hate to break the news to you, but your hottie is a private investigator from Michigan," Mary said to Alice. "And he's meeting us at our next stop, which is a small town about an hour north of here. We're working together on the case. Now get packed up, or I'm leaving without you."

"What about him?" Jason said, pointing at Kurt.

"I don't know, throw some ice on the lobster and get him into the car," Mary said.

Alice waggled a finger at Mary.

"Keep your damn hands off him," Alice said. "I've put too much work into him to have you try to snatch him out of my bed."

"He's married, Alice," Mary said, rolling her eyes. "And I'm sure his interest in you was part of his cover. Like saying he was into plastics."

"Bullshit," Alice said. "That young man may not know it, but I'm gonna rock his damn world."

32.

I snorted coke from off the stripper's ass.
My face looked back from a sheet of pale glass.
            -Eclipse (by Groovy Train)

My favorite part of the drive north to Bucerias was the bars sporting a ten-foot tall bottle of Corona.

There were several of them and they made me feel nostalgic for some reason. Maybe because during the summer in Michigan, cold bottles of Corona were Anna's favorite beverage. With a lime, of course.

Or maybe the roadside bars seemed familiar to me because they looked like relics from the past. They had a 1950s feel to them, like kitschy roadside restaurants from sixty years ago in America.

Being on the road here, in fact, reminded me a lot of what my imagination told me the United States had been like decades ago. It seemed like there were less rules. I saw a motorcycle driven by a man with a woman behind him and a child in the woman's arms.

None of them wore helmets.

At least I had a room waiting for me in Bucerias. I had placed a slightly nervous, slightly urgent call to my travel gal in Grosse Pointe, who had managed to find a place for me to stow my gear and get a decent night's sleep. I had no idea if it was nice, or if I would need to sleep with one eye open.

The murder of Bulldog had been a shock, to say the least. Who had killed him and why?

Was someone else looking for Zack Hatter? It seemed like a ridiculous idea, especially as there are now two private investigators working together on the case.

Could it be there was a third party? One that was willing to kill to get their hands on the Mad Hatter?

I had more questions than answers, unfortunately.

In any event, without lodgings to worry about, my mind naturally turned to another unanswered question. Mary Cooper.

I laughed in spite of myself. She reminded me a little bit of the other women in my life. Both Anna and my sister Ellen were known to be smart-asses. And Mary Cooper seemed to have a personality along those same lines. Although, with Mary, there seemed to be a little bit more of an edge.

There was still some doubt in my mind whether or not I should believe her. Was she really a private investigator in Los Angeles? Maybe she was looking for Zack Hatter for some other reason. An overzealous fan? A lawyer? A bail bondsman?

Still, I kept finding myself wanting to believe her. She seemed genuine, at least with why she was looking for Zack. And if she could help me find him, I wasn't about to complain.

As I got closer to Bucerias I started to get the hang of Mexico traffic. It seemed if you wanted to take a left you had to exit the main road to the right, drive along the street and look for either an intersection or an underpass in order to cross over to the other side.

According to the map on my phone, which surprisingly worked fairly well, I needed to make a left so, naturally, I exited to the right, drove about five hundred feet and saw an underpass. I drove through it, passing three tables of vendors selling stuffed animals, skulls painted the colors of NFL teams and candy.

Eventually, I found my way to a two-story house with a purple door. The number above the door matched the address my travel agent had sent to me via email. There was an open parking spot just past the entrance to the house, next to a stand that was selling tongue tacos.

Interesting.

Tongue tacos.

Sounded like slang for some sort of sex maneuver.

I locked up the rental car and knocked on the door. A woman in an apron showed me to my room, which was in an upstairs hallway with its own bathroom. There was a common area where the woman said dinner was served for the guests. I could smell something cooking and suddenly I realized how hungry I was.

Still, I wanted to at least explore the area. So I threw my bags on the bed, took the key I was supposed to use for the front door and walked outside.

How hard could it be to find Mexican gangsters in Mexico?

33.

It comes for you when knives don't see the light.
It comes for you when blood spills out of night.
            -Part Four (by Groovy Train)

"Put the Human Blister in that room," Mary said. She'd lucked out. A quick call to her client, Connie Hapford, had resulted in impressive digs – a cool house in Bucerias with a view of the ocean. There were at least six rooms, and Mary chose to put Kurt and his horrible sunburn in the room closest to the bathroom. It also happened to be the farthest away from the master bedroom and bathroom that Mary had chosen for herself.

"Wow, check out this bar!" Jason called from the courtyard.

They had passed it quickly en route to getting Kurt situated in his room, but Jason, always open to the possibility of a good time, had stopped at the far end of the pool.

Alice threw a tube of cream at Kurt who was now on his back on the bed. The tube hit him directly on the chest.

"Ow goddamnit!" he yelled.

"Oh shut up," Alice said. "You're probably used to rubbing lotion on yourself."

Alice glanced at Mary. "Let's go get a drink."

She and Mary went down to the courtyard, whose centerpiece was a spectacular saltwater pool bordered with gorgeous Mexican tile. The bar featured six barstools, multiple racks of liquor, sinks and a full-sized fridge.

Jason was working a blender and poured margaritas for the three of them.

Mary took a sip, and then poured the rest of it into the sink. "Wow, Jason. That was the worst margarita I've ever tasted."

"Yeah, I didn't know how to make one."

Alice dumped hers into the sink.

"Let me show you," Alice said.

Mary debated the merits of waiting for a fresh margarita. Instead, she swung down from her barstool.

"Okay, folks," she said. "I've got some stuff to do. Hold down the fort while I'm gone and if Kurt ends up being in too much pain, go ahead and shoot him. We're still in Mexico. No one will care."

"Waste of a bullet," Alice said.

"Can you buy some weed for me?" Jason asked.

"Nope, sure can't," Mary said.

The building had a second courtyard which featured a big wooden door and iron gates. Mary stepped through both and shut them behind her, not just to keep people out, but to keep her dysfunctional gringos from getting loose in town and causing an international incident.

Mary strolled up the street, past a tourism office, a coffee shop, a stand advertising whale watching and a Laundromat. The air was cool and clean, fresher than in PV.

Finally, she came to a side street that led directly to the beach. There was a taxi stand on the corner with half a dozen men sitting around a single white car.

"Buenos tardes, señorita," one of them said.

"Hola," Mary replied.

There were a few murmurs in Spanish but Mary kept walking. At the entrance to the beach was a huge bar, filled with what she instinctively knew were Americans, Canadians or a mixture of both.

Several of them looked up at her as she passed by. The drink board caught her eye. More accurately, the prices caught her eye.

Could they really be that cheap?

She glanced down the row of the bar. She needed just the right kind of person. Probably a guy, but these days you never really knew.

There.

She spotted him at the corner, with his back against the wall. Middle-aged but he looked young. Facial hair, tattoos. Both ears pierced.

She didn't know him, but she knew exactly what kind of guy he was.

Mary made her way to the end of the bar and squeezed in between her target and a guy who would win an award for Most Preppy bar customer.

"Pacifico," Mary said to the bartender who looked like he was about twelve years old not because he was young looking, but because he was in fact twelve years old.

Apparently there were no liquor laws in Mexico.

She got her beer and the man in the corner said, "Put it on my tab, Oscar."

Mary turned to him. "Gracias."

He held up his beer and they clinked glasses.

"Not to be blunt, but do you know anywhere I could get a pick-me-up?" Mary asked. "I just got off the plane and I'm kind of jonesing."

"Not me," he said. "I've been clean for ten years. You oughta try it. You're beautiful, and nothing will ruin your good looks faster than getting hooked on that stuff. But if you've got your mind made up, he can help you."

The man pointed with his bottle to Mr. Preppy. Mary turned to him. Was the guy in the corner serious?

The preppy guy looked at Mary, sensing he had just been the object of a referral.

"Hi, I'm Ward," he said.

He had on a pink Ralph Lauren polo shirt, madras shorts, and leather sandals. A Rolex was on one wrist. He had a pasty face with squinty eyes and delicate hands. His eyes were shifty and she knew that the guy in the corner wasn't kidding.

Not only did it appear Ward sold drugs, he seemed to be a consumer, as well.

"Let's go to my office," Ward said, pointing to an empty table near the beach.

They each took a chair and the boy bartender brought over another beer for Mary and a clear plastic cup for Ward.

"A mojito," Ward said to Mary. "These are killer for these prices. Two-for-one now, you know? And super strong."

Mary hadn't really finished her Pacifico but she tossed it down and grabbed the new bottle. The prices she'd seen on display, she realized, were not only unbelievably cheap, but it was two drinks for one.

Wow, no wonder everyone at the bar seemed blotto.

"So what are you looking for and how do I know you're not a cop?" Ward asked her. He squinted his eyes, like he was trying to be tough. Clint Eastwood in neatly pressed khakis.

She burst out laughing. "A cop? Here in Mexico? How would that even work? Would I be cooperating with the government? The police force? Do they even have one down here?"

Mr. Pink Shirt laughed. "Oh, they have cops. But they only pay attention to you if you forget to pay them."

Mary took a sip of her beer. Ward drank hungrily from his mojito.

"What about Los Zetas?" Mary asked. "Do you have to pay them, too?"

Ward's face turned the same color as his shirt. "Los Zetas? Jesus, no. I stay away from them. I'm just a party guy. Not big-time at all. You get big-time around here, you end up dead. Fast."

Mary pulled out a wad of cash she'd been saving for just this moment.

"I want to buy from you. But just information. If the Zetas had somebody I wanted to find, who would I talk to?"

He shook his head. "They don't do that. They don't hold people. They kill them," he practically hissed at her. His face had gone pale. "Even if they said they were holding someone, which they would never say, they would have already killed them. If you're looking for a person the Zetas have, they're already dead. Save your money. I want nothing to do with you."

He got up and walked back to the bar.

Mary put the money away and turned in her chair to face the Pacific.

It was something she had considered, but ruled out. Now, she had to face the possibility a bit more seriously.

Maybe the Mad Hatter was already dead.

34.

Flesh for cash and booze for hire.
Take your chance and feed my fire.
                    -Blood Shots (by Groovy Train)

He awoke to a couple pieces of good news.

One, it appeared he had survived the drug withdrawals.

He had made it through full, emergency detox that would have killed a lot of people, but he, the Mad Hatter, had fucking survived.

It was nothing short of a miracle.

The other piece of good news was that he felt hopeful.

Maybe the shadow guy with the machete had been part of his detox and wasn't real at all? An imagined phantom.

Imagined Phantoms. What a great name for an album!

Maybe the weird chick in the room by the beach had been imagined, too.

No, he quickly remembered that was real. He had nailed her and the sex had been too real to have been a fantasy. Fantasy sex, dream sex, whatever you want to call it, was too clean and romantic. Real sex was down and dirty with all the accompanying sights, sounds and smells.

They'd definitely had sex.

Weird chick in the room by the beach had been real. For sure.

Now, it was time to get his bearings.

He looked around the room. It was totally empty. Not even a rug. Bare wood floors, plaster walls full of cracks and missing chunks. A window with wooden shutters locked closed with a padlock.

That was all bad news.

Then again, had they locked him up to prevent him from hurting someone else?

It happened before.

One time he'd gotten a big knife during a really bad drunk and his girlfriend at the time had locked him in a closet. The bitch. He never hurt anyone when he was drunk or high. At least not on purpose.

The Hatter was mad, sure, but not a killer.

Really, a harmless drunk and druggie.

Now, he got to his feet and it was a bit of a struggle. His legs felt rubbery and he thought how nice a screwdriver would be. Really cold orange juice, couple shots of vodka, didn't even matter if it was cheap vodka. Hell, potato vodka—

The door banged open and shadow man was back with his machete. He stepped into the room and the shadow disappeared, revealing a scrawny young man, probably in his late teens, with the aforementioned machete. His body was covered with tattoos, easily visible since he wore no shirt, had torn shorts and flip flops. The tattoos went all the way up and around his neck. Zack noted they covered his hands and fingers.

The sight of the young man made his skin crawl.

"Good morning," Zack said, realizing how stupid he sounded. "What's up, man?"

Machete boy stepped aside and revealed the woman he'd screwed in the room by the beach.

She was thicker than he remembered, and when she smiled, he saw her bad teeth.

His penis retracted a bit at the sight of her, but he'd banged a lot worse looking women than this one. Hell, he'd done one who'd been as hairy as a Yeti.

"Hello, lover boy," she said with a thick accent.

Zack's smile was more of a grimace.

And then suddenly, he remembered her name.

"Hello Zeta," he said.

35.

The door slams on a Sunday harmony.
An angel laughs at my sordid memory.
                    -Remember Me (by Groovy Train)

The photo I had of Zack was a good one, quality wise.

After all, there were hundreds upon hundreds of photographs of the guy. From back when he as a star, mostly.

That was the problem.

There weren't many *recent* photos of him. And most of them were when he was onstage. What I really wished I had was a recent photo showing him with all of the wear and tear that comes with being a former rock star.

Still, the photo would at least give people an idea of who I was looking for.

Bucerias was a town that had two distinct areas. There was the highway section with several banks, stores and restaurants, most of it screaming low income. And then there was the beach, with its much more expensive housing and shops.

What was interesting to me was that during the day it seemed like most of the locals were down by the beach, working to tear off their chunk of tourist money.

So that's where I went.

I passed stall after stall of people selling the same stuff. T-shirts with Bucerias on the front. Straw hats. And painted ceramic skulls. Again, a lot of them with NFL team colors painted on them.

It was crazy, but there must have been enough tourist dollars to justify all of these people essentially selling the same stuff.

Without the benefit of being able to speak Spanish, I muddled my way through all of the shopkeepers with Zack Hatter's photograph in front of me. I had used Google's translate to figure out how to ask, but I had simplified it to 'este hombre aqui?' Which basically meant is this man here?

A lot of blank stares, shrugging of shoulders and a few torrents of Spanish followed by a hawking of their goods in English.

The people were friendly, but not in the least bit helpful.

Parallel to the ocean, the shops ran uninterrupted until there was a town square of sorts, with a huge sculpture of a man diving for oysters. From there, the vendors fanned out and the air was filled with the smell of food cooking. Barbecue and it smelled fantastic.

I also saw some fruit stands and a bread stand. Meat and bread was all I needed. Whenever I cooked at home, Anna would always sigh and throw some peas in the microwave or put together a salad real fast. When I planned a meal, I focused on the two main food groups: meat and bread. And if I had time, I usually included a third: cheese.

Around the square I went, showing the photo of Hatter, drawing blank stares. I noticed a huge restaurant with an enormous patio. Even though I'd avoided the tourists, I figured I could get a ton of them with one shot. So I asked the tables if they'd seen Hatter.

No one had.

"Try the bar upstairs," one patron said. "It's full of Canadians. They're nosy bastards."

I glanced up, saw a big advertising banner proudly claiming the establishment's penchant for broadcasting hockey games.

There was a separate entrance to the bar to the left of the restaurant and I used it, climbed the stairs and went into the bar. I saw a chalkboard advertising a bucket of six beers for eighty pesos. That was less than five bucks by my rough math.

My kinda place.

Maybe the Hatter's too?

Along the balcony overlooking the town square I showed the photo, again to no avail. But when I got to the bar, where it looked to me like the hardcore drinkers were stationed, one guy nodded in recognition.

"Yep, he was here. Drunk as hell," the guy said. He had on shorts and a T-shirt that was way too tight. He'd either washed it and it had shrunk, or he'd gained weight. Judging by the empty beer bottles in front of him, I was guessing the latter.

"Or maybe he was stoned, it was hard to tell," the man continued. "He looked familiar. But now that I see the photo that's Zack Hatter, isn't it?"

"It sure is. Was he here alone?"

"He started here alone, but he ended up leaving with a local. A woman."

There was something about the way he said it.

"Did you know her?"

He held up his hands and acted like I'd accused him of drug trafficking. "No, no. Not me. No way."

"Well, do you know her name? Where she lives?"

"Sure, everyone knows her name," the man said. He lowered his head and sort of whispered to me. "She's the biggest hooker in Bucerias."

He said the name and the case suddenly spun in a whole new direction.

"Her name is Zeta."

36.

Slap some steel around your wrist,
Answer truth and swing your fist.
            -Bad Cop (by Groovy Train)

It hadn't taken Rutger long to locate the first of the local hoods.

After that, it didn't take much more time to trail the punk to where the rest of the gang was hanging out.

He knew Los Zetas controlled this area and that there was no way an entire gang would be working in Bucerias without the Zetas' knowledge.

Before he'd plugged Bulldog, he'd gotten the slob to cough up Bucerias and the Zetas.

It made sense.

Zack Hatter was a known drug user and the Zetas made their money trafficking narcotics. Easy to put two and two together and realize the Zetas must have grabbed Hatter, hoping for a bigger payday down the road.

Kidnapping was very much still alive and well in Mexico. In fact, one time he'd killed a lawyer from Chicago, dumped the body in the ocean, and then staged it to appear as if the lawyer had been kidnapped. He'd even read that the family had paid some Mexican gang millions of dollars.

Dumb bastards.

Unfortunately for the Zetas, they'd now grabbed the guy Rutger needed. He was here to grab Zack Hatter, get some information from him for Mr. Hmm, and then kill him.

So this time, the Zetas were the ones who were going to have to pay.

It was up to them how many of them would pay with their short, unhappy lives.

All Rutger had done once he'd arrived in Bucerias was to ask the guys at the taxi stand where he could buy the highest quality weed. They'd referred him to an area north of where all of the tourist market stands were located.

Once there, Rutger had picked out a dealer immediately. After that, he'd stalked the guy until he'd sold all of his merchandise and gone back for more supply, which turned out to be a run-down, dumpy apartment building on the edge of town. There weren't really any tourists over here, so Rutger took great care to stay in his rental car and change locations often.

Eventually, a small group left the building led by a guy who Rutger immediately pegged as the alpha of the group.

Alphas can always pick out other alphas a mile away.

Rutger trailed the crew onto the highway and then off a side road. He checked behind him. There was no other traffic, no risk of being disturbed.

He slid his gun out and held it with one hand and then pulled the rental car out and even with the dusty, dirty white truck being driven by the crew.

Rutger slammed the car into their truck and forced them to the side of the road.

Rutger got out, the gun behind his back, with a map in the other hand.

"Donde Puerto Vallarta?" he asked, acting lost and confused.

Where is Puerto Vallarta?

The driver of the truck wasn't the leader of the gang, so he got out and Rutger could see him reaching for a gun.

Not yet too worried about the lost gringo tourist asking for directions. But he was pissed and no doubt his boss had told him to get rid of this annoyance and fast.

Rutger could see all of that in the man's demeanor.

The group's boss was in the passenger seat, looking bored. Rutger moved the map closer to him and then drew his pistol and fired through the large square of paper. The bullet caught the driver in the forehead and blew out most of the back of his head. The driver folded and sagged to the ground, one hand clinging to the door of the truck.

The man in the passenger seat hadn't moved.

Rutger stepped up and pointed the gun at him.

"Zack Hatter. Donde esta?"

"Quien eres?" the gang leader asked. *Who are you?*

The man looked at him with a blank expression so Rutger shot him in the knee.

The man reached into the footwell of the truck and started to come up with an ancient Mac-10 submachine gun.

Rutger shot him in the shoulder.

The gun dropped and Rutger reached inside the truck, took the gun away, then dragged the man out and dumped him onto the ground.

"Donde?" Rutger repeated. *Where?*

The man on the ground unleashed another torrent of Spanish. Rutger understood that he was saying he didn't know anything. *No se. Nada.*

It was frustrating.

People never wanted to talk.

Rutger shot him in the head.

He knew he wouldn't be getting anything out of the man, so instead he would do some detective work and look inside the truck.

He found a brown bag with a half-eaten tortilla and refried beans. A large Styrofoam cup filled with lemonade and a brochure for a tourist attraction that included caves.

And a ballpoint pen.

The ballpoint pen had been used to circled one of the buildings near the caves.

Aha, Rutger thought.

A cave.

Of course.

37.

She stuck her toes into the sand,
Nails into my head.
She walked along the razor's edge,
And toasted all our dead.
        -Martini Beach (by Groovy Train)

Mary had a hunch. Mr. Preppy claimed he didn't know, but she felt her instincts about the guy in the corner weren't wrong.

So once Ward left in a huff, leaving Mary with his dire warning about the Zetas killing all of their hostages, she went back to the bar where the guy in the corner was still watching her.

"How'd it go?" he asked, with a small smile.

"Not good," Mary said. "He didn't have what I needed."

She set her Pacifico on the bar and stuck out her hand. "Name's Mary, by the way."

"Hello, Mary-By-The-Way. Name's Neil. I'm judging by the look in your eye that you might think I have what you need, is that right?"

"Possibly," she admitted. "I need information." She had an image of Zack Hatter on her phone and she showed it to Neil. "I'm looking for him. He's missing and the rumor is the Zetas have him."

"I suspect that rumor's wrong," Neil said.

"Why's that?"

"The Zetas don't kidnap. They kill. Plus, that guy looks like he's been around the block. No way he's getting involved with them."

Neil peered closer at the photograph. "Besides," he added. "That dude's a dead ringer for Zack Hatter from Groovy Train."

"It is Zack Hatter from Groovy Train."

"No shit? That's cool," Neil said. "Do you know him?"

"Not really."

"Well, your rumor is definitely wrong. Zetas hate publicity. No way they'd snatch him."

Mary put her phone away and took a long drink from her beer. It was possible the rumor was wrong. But why would Bulldog lie? Why would he say the Zetas have Zack?

She thought about it. What was the connection between the little town of Bucerias, home of oyster divers, and the music industry in Puerto Vallarta?

Drugs was the easy answer.

Zack was famous for drugs.

And women.

A thought hit Mary out of the blue.

She turned to Neil. "What about hookers?"

He laughed and nodded his head.

"Sure, I was just thinking that," Neil said. "If there was one woman who would have found her way to Zack Hatter, it would be her."

"Who?"

"Zeta."

38.

Hey now, hey now, bring that monkey shine.
Hey now, hey now, show me your evenin' grind.
        -Hazel (by Groovy Train)

I put in a call to Mary and she answered on the first ring.

"Zeta's a hooker," she said before I could even get a word out.

"I know."

"No you didn't," she said.

"I did. I talked to some Canadians at a bar who said they saw Zack with her."

"Wow, great minds think alike," she said. "Did you get an address for her?"

"I have a general area, how about you?"

"Same. Let's meet and go together."

We figured out we were only about four blocks apart so less than a minute later we joined forces near the taxi stand, which seemed to be the unofficial hub of the little town.

The six guys watching the one white car all nodded at me as I walked past. I wondered if they made any money or if they just liked hanging out together.

Mary approached from the beach and all of the guys suddenly sat up straighter.

She was a good-looking woman, I had to admit, and I couldn't blame the guys for wanting to get a better look.

"How far away is the general area?" she asked.

"Not far at all," I said. "Supposedly it's a condo complex called Isle Verde. Just a few blocks from here."

"Great, let's go," Mary said. We turned down the street, and I led the way to my rental car.

"I wish I had a gun, though," she said.

"Me, too."

We walked together and I told her about my meeting with the Canadians. She filled me in on her conversation with the preppy drug dealer.

"Not gonna lie," I said. "I'm glad we didn't have to pursue the Los Zetas angle. I have no interest in dealing with those guys."

"Yeah, they seem like a fun bunch of dudes," Mary said. "I heard they're big fans of burning people alive. You know, when they're bored and need some entertainment. As opposed to, you know, watching Netflix or something."

"The shows are probably too violent for them," I said.

We couldn't miss the sign to Isle Verde.

It was a huge white monstrosity with a logo that looked like it'd been developed in the seventies. Next to the name on the sign was a pair of palm trees, but one of them was crooked and looked like it had been toppled by high winds.

Not a great message to send to potential residents.

The complex itself looked like maybe it had been impressive at one point, but now the upkeep had gotten to be too much for the current owners. I saw peeling plaster, a parking area choked with weeds and a tile roof with plenty of pieces missing.

"The hooking business has seen better times, apparently," Mary said. "Let's ring some bells."

She stepped up to the main doors to the complex and opened them. I followed her inside.

There was a security guard asleep in a chair. Mary let out a low whistle until his eyes opened.

She pulled out a wad of pesos and held it in front of him.

"Zeta," she said.

He took the money.

"Trescientos cinco."

I knew enough Spanish to translate. 305.

We took the elevator up and knocked on the door. The hallway smelled of mildew and fajitas.

The door opened and a thin woman with long brown hair and smeared makeup answered. She looked like she'd either just had sex, used drugs, or both.

"Hablas ingles?" I asked.

"A little," she answered.

"We're looking for Zeta," Mary said. "Do you know where she is?"

The woman yawned. "Los Meranos."

"What the hell is that?" Mary asked.

"A zip line," the woman said. She pronounced it 'zeep line.' "You know, wheeeeee!!!!" She imitated someone riding on a zip line.

"She went zip lining?" I asked. "A hooker on a zip line. One of my fantasies during puberty."

"I can't take you anywhere, can I?" Mary asked me.

"And they have cuevas there," the woman said.

"Cuevas?" I asked. "What the hell are cuevas?"

The woman nodded and started to close the door as she gave us the translation.

"Caves."

39.

Lines along the sky above and rumors down below.
Watch the hookers walk the street putting on a show.
-Stiletto Groove (by Groovy Train)

During his years working for organized crime, Rutger had come to the conclusion that the average citizen would probably be shocked to learn how many of the legitimate businesses they frequented were in fact owned by the Mob.

In New York, he knew of a candy store, a miniature golf course, an ice cream chain and a Zumba studio that were all owned by organized crime.

But he if were to tell the truth, he couldn't say that he'd ever seen a zip line business owned by criminals.

It was a first.

Although, once he thought about it, it made sense.

Anywhere there was cash, there was fertile ground for illegal behavior. Whether it was not reporting income to the government, or using the business as a place to launder money, tourist traps could serve a key role in the business of the underworld.

Now, he steered his rental car into the parking lot of Los Meranos Zip Line Park.

There were plenty of signs around for confused tourists pointing them in the direction of the zip line, the restaurant, the petting zoo and finally, the entrance to the caves.

The hunter in him was excited.

He was close, he knew that.

Rutger could practically sense his quarry nearby and although his task wasn't necessarily to kill Zack Hatter, at least not right away, Rutger's blood thirst was intensifying.

Along with the excitement came a surge of caution.

This is when mistakes happened. When aggression overcame thoughtfulness and errors in judgment occurred. The kind that got people killed. Even highly talented specialists like Rutger himself.

He'd seen it too many times. And when he'd first gotten into the profession, he'd almost made the mistake.

Once.

After that, he'd never let himself get careless again.

So he paused and thought.

If someone had grabbed Zack Hatter, would they really be holding him in a cave system frequented by tourists? It could mean a lot of witnesses. Plus, tourism was big business here. The government wouldn't want messy violence anywhere near where the tourists hung out.

If it was in the ghetto, fine.

But not where it would cost everyone money.

So was it possible Zack Hatter was really being held here? The easy answer was only if the cave system was owned by the same criminals who took Hatter.

Rutger gave it 50-50 odds.

He carefully examined the cars in the parking lot, a gaggle of tourists waiting to go into the zip line entrance.

The place looked legitimate on the surface.

Still, he was wary.

He put his experience to good use.

In nearly all of the legitimate businesses owned by criminals, Rutger knew there was always a place that was off-limits to all but a few. This was so innocent employees or delivery men, or even customers, wouldn't see something they shouldn't have and end up dead because of it.

The same would be the case here.

His first thought was that a cave system would be a perfect place to hold someone. Underground. Perhaps a section blocked off from the others.

But then it raised its own problems. What about a bathroom? Coming and going? Meals, if they were feeding him?

It seemed like a pain in the ass.

He needed to start at the head of the snake. An office. There was always an office in these places. And often, there would be a second office. The real headquarters for the real business.

And if Rutger was wrong, and Zack Hatter was actually in a fucking cave somewhere, he figured he would find someone in the office who could take him there.

He got out of the car, locked it, and patted his front pocket for the extra clip he might need. The gun, with its silencer now reattached, was in his waistband at the small of his back.

You never knew in situations like this.

There was a separate, small parking lot behind the main one, with a sign that said authorized parking only.

This is where the staff would park.

He walked over to it, passed the sign and continued around behind the main building. He saw dumpsters and the back door that clearly led to the restaurant. To the left was a section of building with its own private entrance, and a Mazda sports car parked near the door.

The Mazda seemed out of place and Rutger felt another surge of excitement.

He walked up to the door, reached for the doorknob and turned it.

It opened.

A thin, scrawny guy in a white tank top and tattoos sat with his feet up on a desk in front of him, smoking a joint. A woman sat in a chair across from him and she turned in her chair and looked back at Rutger.

A machete was on the desk.

"Zeta?" Rutger asked the woman.

"Si," she responded.

Rutger brought out his gun and casually shot Tattoo Boy in the head.

Zeta didn't move.

She looked at the machete, and instantly thought better of it.

Rutger walked over to her, put the muzzle of the gun against her temple.

"Where's Zack Hatter?" he asked.

40.

My woman's got a turtleneck,
She wears it all in black.
My woman's got a nylon heart
It beats the others back.
               -Black Turtleneck (by Groovy Train)

"Puberty must have been very difficult for you," Mary said. "A hooker and a zip line? That's kind of an unusual fantasy."

"It may not have been exactly that," John said. "But I did tend to get very creative."

They had left Zeta's apartment building and gotten on the road to the zip line/cave complex. Mary wasn't sure what to expect.

This case had gotten awfully weird, awfully fast.

She was glad to be away from the rest of the Coopers, though, and she found hanging out with John Rockne to be tolerable.

Maybe even somewhat enjoyable.

Mary shook her head. This guy was a trip. She liked him, liked his easygoing personality and the fact that he had a sense of humor was a plus.

Too bad he was married. Or maybe that was a good thing.

"What about you?" he asked. "Or are you still going through puberty?"

"No, I'm all done," Mary said. "Just wrapped up puberty a couple of weeks ago. It felt good, but it was brief. No elaborate fantasies other than clear skin."

"That's great, you being done with puberty, and all," John said.

"Thanks, that means a lot."

The highway was crowded with the usual array of bad drivers, trucks loaded with landscape supplies and the occasional suicidal motorcyclist going way too fast.

"So what do you think?" Mary said. "Do you think we'll actually find Zack Hatter at a zip line place for tourists?"

"Probably not," Rockne said. "But it's worth checking out, if nothing more than to cross it off the list. It does make you wonder, though, if he's not out there, what is Zeta the hooker doing out there? Can she really meet a lot of johns at a zip line business? What's her pitch? Get off the zip line, climb onto me?"

"That's a good slogan," Mary said. "But you're right. Most of the men out here are going to be tourists with their families. Hookers work in bars and online. What is she doing out here?"

John didn't have an answer and Mary let the question hang in the silence. The road wound up into the hills and soon they could no longer get any glimpses of the Pacific.

"So what's your wife like?" Mary asked.

John raised an eyebrow and looked at her. "Feisty," he said. "A lot like you."

Mary scoffed. "I'm not feisty," she said. "I'm lively. So you have kids?"

"Two girls," John said. "It's weird being away from them." He glanced at Mary. "How about you?"

"Yes, I find it weird being away from you, too," she said.

"Married? Kids?"

"Not married. No kids. At least, as far as I know."

Old joke, but Mary always used it to deflect the question.

Somewhat gratefully, Mary saw a sign for the turnoff to the zip line, and a parking lot ahead.

John pulled the rental car into the driveway. To the right, she could see a cluster of buildings with people milling around wearing helmets and harnesses, either just back from a zip line ride, or about to depart.

To the left, was another building and a smaller parking lot.

"Park there," she said to John, pointing toward the smaller lot. "That looks like an office in back. Let's go see if anyone knows what the hell is going on."

John parked and together they walked to the office.

There was a red Mazda parked near the door, and another car next to it. Mary thought it looked like a rental car, too.

She wished again she had a gun.

Mary knocked and heard people moving on the other side of the door. Her hand instinctively went to where she carried her gun. She started to say something to John, but just then the door opened.

Mary turned her head back to the door but a hand shot out, grabbed her by the hair, and yanked her inside.

41.

We wander in from the other side.
We wonder how we lost our pride.
                    -Mess (by Groovy Train)

It was probably stupid to do so, but I crashed in through the door, following Mary. It seemed pointless to do anything else. What was I going to do, duck around the corner, call 911 and hope someone arrived?

So I barged in after Mary.

The first thing I saw was a dead guy in a chair, with blood all over his face and half of his head gone.

There was a woman on her knees with her arms folded over her head and directly in front of me was a tall thin man with dark hair and a face that betrayed no emotion whatsoever.

He had a gun held to Mary's head.

He was looking at me with a quizzical expression on his face.

And finally, slumped on the ground next to the woman with her arms folded over her head was Zack Hatter.

"Jesus, can we fit a few more people in here?" the man with the gun said. His face showed no humor, but his mouth was shaped into a small grimace.

"Did you say Jesus or Jésus?" Mary asked.

"Who the hell are you?" I asked.

"I'm the guy that's going to kill everyone in this room if Mr. Zack Hatter doesn't tell me what I need to know."

He pushed Mary across the room to where Zack and the woman on her knees were, and then he waved me over there, too, with his gun.

"Well, this sucks," Mary said.

"But I still haven't found what I'm looking for," Zack sang, in the melody of the song by U2. He looked deranged. He was either drunk, on drugs, or out of his mind from pain and suffering.

He looked even worse than he did in the horrible photos. I knew it was him, but I swear to God he looked like what Zack Hatter's grandpa would look like. Ancient. And very much the worse for wear.

The thin man with the gun had a cell phone in his hand. He looked closely at Zack.

"I'd kill you if you weren't brain-dead already," he said.

He looked around the room. "Bad news for you folks."

"It *is* crowded in here," I said. "How about I leave and make room for everyone?" I said as I put my hand on the doorknob, but it opened without any effort on my part and a shotgun barrel entered the room, followed by three men covered in tattoos, heavily armed and they trained all of their guns on the slim man with the pistol. There was nowhere for any of us to go, including the thin man with the pistol, who the new visitors seemed to be concentrating on.

"Señor, la pistola, por favor," the guy with the shotgun said.

178

"No way, José," the thin man said.

He fired, casually, almost without aiming and the guy with the shotgun staggered back, but he was able to pull the trigger and the shotgun erupted. The thin man's chest was extremely thin now as the shotgun blast disintegrated it and turned into a shredded mass of blood and tissue. His pistol swung as he sagged and it fired again, this time sending a round through the kneeling woman's head.

More blood and a fine mist filled the air.

"Holy shit," I said. I squeezed closer to Zack and Mary. I had no choice. My ears were ringing and the room was filled with the battling scents of gunfire and death.

"Fucking A!" Zack Hatter exclaimed. "No encore tonight, folks!" His eyes were wild and he slumped forward onto the ground.

One of the other newcomers, with a shotgun of his own, walked over to where the thin man on the ground with the destroyed chest lay writhing.

"You killed my brother, cabron" he said, his voice in a thick accent. He jacked a shell into the shotgun's chamber, placed the end of the barrel inches from the man's face and pulled the trigger.

I looked away from the destruction it created, and looked the man in the eye.

He looked straight at me, then Mary and then Zack.

"Forget this, or you die."

"No problema," Mary said.

The leader turned to the other guy. "Llevar los cuerpos."

The third guy dragged his dead companion from the room, and then both he and the other man hauled out the thin man and the dead woman, who I figured was Zeta.

I was just guessing, but I figured the thin man had been the shooter in Puerto Vallarta, the guy who'd killed Bulldog.

But who was he working for? And what had he wanted from Zack?

The thought of Zack made me look down at the former rock star.

He was drooling onto the floor and it smelled like he'd soiled himself.

Last week.

When we heard the vehicles outside leave with engines roaring and tires spinning, Mary nudged Zack with her foot.

"Rise and shine, superstar," she said.

A little bit of vomit seeped from his mouth.

"Maybe we should get him to a doctor," I said.

"If they need a stool sample, it smells like he's already got one in his pants," Mary noted.

42.

I wish I had another day
To tell you why I didn't pray.
I wish I had another lie
To sing to you a lullaby.
               -I Wish (by Groovy Train)

"So what the hell happened?" Mary asked.

We were both standing in Zack's hospital room. It was simple, but clean. It even had a window, which showed just a slice of the ocean, and a decent view of the mountains, now slightly shrouded in mist.

We'd pooled the rest of our expense money and bribed our way into a decent hotel with a good room.

Mary and I needed information from Zack. After all, we both had clients waiting for word from us.

I knew Mary had already called her client, Connie Hapford, and I had touched base with Sunny Hatter, letting her know that Zack was fine and that his latest adventure in Mexico was over.

Still, I had a feeling he wasn't out of the woods just yet.

After all, there was a third party apparently *very* interested in something Zack Hatter had.

Zack was sitting up in bed, an IV in his arm. He really looked like hell. And old. He looked every one of his years, with a deep tan, sharply etched lines in his face but his blue eyes still held some power, now that he was out of the grips of whatever drugs he'd been on.

There was still some charisma that even the long years and nights full of booze and drugs hadn't managed to diminish.

"How the hell would I know?" Zack said, finally answering Mary's question. His voice was raw but still had a presence. It seemed to fill the room. "One minute, I'm partying, having sex with what's her name, and then the next minute, I wake up in that room and some guy is waving a machete at me and that bitch keeps drugging me up. What the hell!"

"So was Zeta holding you for the guy with the gun?" Mary asked.

"Zeta?" Zack said. "Who the hell is Zeta."

"The hooker," I patiently explained. "Your date for the last few days."

"Phooey," Zack said. "My date. I can't believe I dipped my love wand into that."

"Please, Zack," Mary said. "Stick to the topic at hand."

"How the hell would I know?" Zack said. "I don't know what her fricking plan was. She said she was in love with me and wanted to go on the road with me. I get that a lot. I was already plastered by then. She didn't look too bad. But, man, when I sobered up and saw her, my grass snake curled back up into my pants and started hibernating."

It seemed like Zack enjoyed talking about his privates.

"What about the guy with the gun?" I asked. "He said you needed to tell him where he could find what he was looking for."

Zack Hatter suddenly sported a look of disgust. "Who knows what that asshole wanted."

"I think you do," Mary said. "And you're going to tell us otherwise we'll make sure you go to prison for all those murders back there."

Wow, I was impressed. Mary Cooper was a badass. I knew she was bluffing, but still, it sounded good. And apparently it scared the hell out of Zack.

"Prison? I can't do prison. Shit, I'm way too good looking."

"Zack," I said. "What did he want."

He finally seemed to collapse in on himself and looked at the ceiling, then shook his head in resignation.

He let out a long breath.

"Have you ever heard of *The Lake House Album*?"

The name rang a bell with me. "Isn't that some kind of bootleg record?"

He looked at me as if I'd insulted him. "Some kind of bootleg? Are you fucking kidding me? It's *the* bootleg. It's the Holy Fucking Grail of bootlegs. Better than Dylan's basement tapes."

Mary nodded. "I remember reading about it. Some legendary meeting between Groovy Train and a bunch of famous musicians who are dead. It's never been found, right?"

"Yeah." He said it without much conviction.

"That's what he wanted you to give him?" I asked. "Do you have it?"

Zack practically leapt off the bed at me.

"Of course I don't have it! Are you nuts?" he shouted. "That thing is worth millions! Do you know how much someone could make off that record? Christ!"

"Do you know where it is?" Mary asked. "Is that what the skinny guy with the gun wanted? The album's location?"

"Not really," Zack said, suddenly going coy again.

"What's that supposed to mean?" Mary asked. She turned to me.

"Should we just shoot him?"

A nurse came in and checked Zack's vital signs. "Can I drink alcohol?" he asked her. "Tequila, nurse?" he asked her. She scowled at him and left.

"Talk about shitty service," he said.

"It's a hospital, not a hotel," I pointed out.

"Whatever, room service is room service. Losers."

I walked over to where the IV was going into his arm.

"What are you doing?" he asked, looking at me.

"Tell us what the guy with the gun wanted to know. It does us no good to bring you back to Los Angeles if someone is going to be waiting there to do this whole thing over again."

"You know," Mary said. "Technically, that might work to our advantage. We take him back, get paid, someone snatches him again, and we get hired again. More money for us."

Zack held up his hands. He'd heard enough.

"Look, okay, I'll be honest. I don't know where it is or even if it actually exists."

"What the hell is that supposed to mean?" I asked.

"We did record a bunch of tracks, I know that. I was there, Jim Morrison, Hendrix stopped by, a bunch of others. I was stoned to the gills, man," Zack said. He looked out the window, remembering. "I remember the music was awesome, though. I *felt* it, you know what I mean? That's the ultimate test. If you feel the music."

"I feel like throwing you out the window," Mary said. "Get to the goddamned point."

"If the tracks have survived all this time, there's only one person in the world who would know where it is. He was the only one sober when we were all jamming together at the lake house. But I haven't spoken to him in twenty-five years because I hate his guts and he hates mine. Neither one of us has ever admitted to the recordings because it might mean we would have to see each other again."

"Who is it?"

"Jimmy King," Zack said, his mouth turning up in a snarl of distaste. "Our bass player. A great bass player, maybe the best ever. But an absolute sonofabitch."

There was a pause.

I looked at Mary.

Mary looked at me.

"Well, we were hired to find you," Mary said. "I'm supposed to bring you back to Los Angeles."

"Me too," I added.

"I'm not going back," Zack said. "I'm going to Michigan."

"Michigan?" I said. "That's where I'm going. That's where I live. Why in the hell would you be going to Michigan?"

"Because that's where Jimmy lives. Northern Michigan. In the woods somewhere."

"You haven't spoken to him in twenty-five years. Why are you going?"

"Because that psychopath with a gun said that he was hired to find me and get the location of the album and then kill me. And he said that his employer hired a killer to go after Jimmy, too. I've got to get to Michigan and warn him."

Mary threw up her hands.

"Call him," she said. "Email him. Call the cops. You don't have to go there in person."

"Jimmy's crazy," Zack said. "He won't listen to anyone but me."

He looked at us.

"And I want to hire you two to come with me."

"No," Mary said.

"You're a team, right?" he asked.

"Hell no!" Mary and I said in unison.

"I've got money," he said. "Lots. Look, who are you working for?"

"Connie Hapford," Mary said.

Zack nodded. "That's no problem, then. I'm her boss and you're fired."

"What about you?" he asked me. "Who hired you? Sunny?"

"Yep," I said.

"Okay, well, she's using my money to pay you, so you're fired, too. Now, whatever your fees are, I'll double them. You can both come with me to Michigan. We'll find Jimmy, see if he has the album, and then we'll go to the cops. In that order."

"I've got other clients," Mary said.

"Yeah, so do I."

Now the drunk and disheveled Zack Hatter was gone. His eyes practically blazed at us from the bed.

"Now listen, you punks," he said. "You were there in that room when three people were killed. I've got no problem telling the Mexican cops I saw you shoot those three. I'm sure they wouldn't care about the gringo, but the two Mexicans? They don't like Americans coming down here and slaughtering the locals."

I looked at Zack, and then back at Mary.

A little smile tugged at the corner of her mouth. "Did you say double my normal rate?" she asked Zack.

"Absolutely," he answered.

They both looked at me.

ABOUT THE AUTHOR

Dan Ames is an international bestselling author and winner of the Independent Book Award for Crime Fiction. You can learn more about him at **www.authordanames.com**

Made in the USA
Lexington, KY
05 October 2017